Robinson
Crusoe

魯賓遜漂流記

商務印書館

This Chinese edition of *Robinson Crusoe*
has been published with the written permission of
Black Cat Publishing.

The copyright of this Chinese edition is owned by
The Commercial Press (H.K.) Ltd.

Name of Book: Robinson Crusoe
Author: Daniel Defoe
Text adaptation: Maud Jackson
Notes and activities: Guglielmo Corrado
Introduction and dossiers: Gina D.B. Clemen
Editors: Rebecca Raynes, Monika Marszewska
Design: Nadia Maestri
Illustrations: Alfredo Belli
Edition: ©2000 Black Cat Publishing
          an imprint of Cideb Editrice, Genoa, Canterbury

系 列 名：Black Cat 優質英語階梯閱讀 · Level 6
書　　名：魯賓遜漂流記
責任編輯：黃淑嫻
封面設計：張　毅　曹　磊
出　　版：商務印書館（香港）有限公司
　　　　　香港筲箕灣耀興道 3 號東滙廣場 8 樓
　　　　　http://www.commercialpress.com.hk
發　　行：香港聯合書刊物流有限公司
　　　　　香港新界大埔汀麗路 36 號中華商務印刷大廈 3 字樓
印　　刷：中華商務彩色印刷有限公司
　　　　　香港新界大埔汀麗路 36 號中華商務印刷大廈
版　　次：2013 年 5 月第 1 版第 3 次印刷
　　　　　© 商務印書館（香港）有限公司
　　　　　ISBN 978 962 07 1670 6
　　　　　Printed in Hong Kong

版權所有　　不得翻印

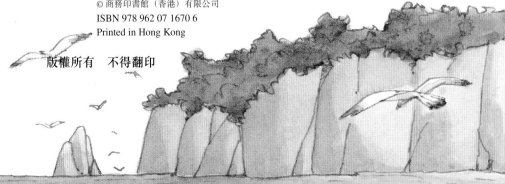

出版説明

　　本館一向倡導優質閱讀，近年來連續推出了以"Q"為標識的
"Quality English Learning 優質英語學習"系列，其中《讀名著學英語》叢
書，更是香港書展入選好書，讀者反響令人鼓舞。推動社會閱讀風氣，推
動英語經典閱讀，藉閱讀拓廣世界視野，提高英語水平，已經成為一種潮
流。

　　然良好閱讀習慣的養成非一日之功，大多數初、中級程度的讀者，常
視直接閱讀厚重的原著為畏途。如何給年輕的讀者提供切實的指引和幫
助，如何既提供優質的學習素材，又提供名師的教學方法，是當下社會關
注的重要問題。針對這種情況，本館特別延請香港名校名師，根據多年豐
富的教學經驗，精選海外適合初、中級英語程度讀者的優質經典讀物，有
系統地出版了這套叢書，名為《Black Cat 優質英語階梯閱讀》。

　　《Black Cat 優質英語階梯閱讀》體現了香港名校名師堅持經典學習的
教學理念，以及多年行之有效的學習方法。既有經過改寫和縮寫的經典名
著，又有富創意的現代作品；既有精心設計的聽、説、讀、寫綜合練習，
又有豐富的歷史文化知識；既有彩色插圖、繪圖和照片，又有英美專業演
員朗讀作品的 CD。適合口味不同的讀者享受閱讀之樂，欣賞經典之美。

　　《Black Cat 優質英語階梯閱讀》由淺入深，逐階提升，好像參與一個
尋寶遊戲，入門並不難，但要真正尋得寶藏，需要投入，更需要堅持。只
有置身其中的人，才能體味純正英語的魅力，領略得到真寶的快樂。當英
語閱讀成為自己生活的一部分，英語水平的提高自然水到渠成。

商務印書館 (香港) 有限公司
編輯部

使用說明 _____

1 應該怎樣選書？

按閱讀興趣選書

《Black Cat 優質英語階梯閱讀》精選世界經典作品，也包括富於創意的現代作品；既有膾炙人口的小說、戲劇，又有非小說類的文化知識讀物，品種豐富，內容多樣，適合口味不同的讀者挑選自己感興趣的書，享受閱讀的樂趣。

按英語程度選書

《Black Cat 優質英語階梯閱讀》現設 Level 1 至 Level 6，由淺入深，涵蓋初、中級英語程度。讀物分級採用了國際上通用的劃分標準，主要以詞彙（vocabulary）和結構（structures）劃分。

Level 1 至 Level 3 出現的詞彙較淺顯，相對深的核心詞彙均配上中文解釋，節省讀者查找詞典的時間，以專心理解正文內容。在註釋的幫助下，讀者若能流暢地閱讀正文內容，就不用擔心這一本書程度過深。

Level 1 至 Level 3 出現的動詞時態形式和句子結構比較簡單。動詞時態形式以現在時（present simple）、現在時進行式（present continuous）、過去時（past simple）為主，句子結構大部分是簡單句（simple sentences）。此外，還包括比較級和最高級（comparative and superlative forms）、可數和不可數名詞（countable and uncountable nouns）以及冠詞（articles）等語法知識點。

Level 4 至 Level 6 出現的動詞時態形式，以現在完成時（present perfect）、現在完成時進行式（present perfect continuous）、過去完成時（past perfect continuous）為主，句子結構大部分是複合句（compound sentences）、條件從句（1st and 2nd conditional sentences）等。此外，還包括情態動詞（modal verbs）、被動形式（passive forms）、動名詞（gerunds）、

短語動詞（phrasal verbs）等語法知識點。

　　根據上述的語法範圍，讀者可按自己實際的英語水平，如詞彙量、語法知識、理解能力、閱讀能力等自主選擇，不再受制於學校年級劃分或學歷高低的約束，完全根據個人需要選擇合適的讀物。

② 怎樣提高閱讀效果？

　　閱讀的方法主要有兩種：一是泛讀，二是精讀。兩者各有功能，適當地結合使用，相輔相成，有事半功倍之效。

　　泛讀，指閱讀大量適合自己程度（可稍淺，但不能過深）、不同內容、風格、體裁的讀物，但求明白內容大意，不用花費太多時間鑽研細節，主要作用是多接觸英語，減輕對它的生疏感，鞏固以前所學過的英語，讓腦子在潛意識中吸收詞彙用法、語法結構等。

　　精讀，指小心認真地閱讀內容精彩、組織有條理、遣詞造句又正確的作品，着重點在於理解"準確"及"深入"，欣賞其精彩獨到之處。精讀時，可充分利用書中精心設計的練習，學習掌握有用的英語詞彙和語法知識。精讀後，可再花十分鐘朗讀其中一小段有趣的文字，邊唸邊細心領會文字的結構和意思。

　　《Black Cat 優質英語階梯閱讀》中的作品均值得精讀，如時間有限，不妨嘗試每兩個星期泛讀一本，輔以每星期挑選書中一章精彩的文字精讀。要學好英語，持之以恆地泛讀和精讀英文是最有效的方法。

③ 本系列的練習與測試有何功能？

　　《Black Cat 優質英語階梯閱讀》特別注重練習的設計，為讀者考慮周到，切合實用需求，學習功能強。每章後均配有訓練聽、説、讀、寫四項技能的練習，分量、難度恰到好處。

聽力練習分兩類，一是重聽故事回答問題，二是聆聽主角對話、書信朗讀、或模擬記者訪問後寫出答案，旨在以生活化的練習形式逐步提高聽力。每本書均配有 CD 提供作品朗讀，朗讀者都是專業演員，英國作品由英國演員錄音，美國作品由美國演員錄音，務求增加聆聽的真實感和感染力。多聆聽英式和美式英語兩種發音，可讓讀者熟悉二者的差異，逐漸培養分辨英美發音的能力，提高聆聽理解的準確度。此外，模仿錄音朗讀故事或模仿主人翁在戲劇中的對白，都是訓練口語能力的好方法。

閱讀理解練習形式多樣化，有縱橫字謎、配對、填空、字句重組等等，注重訓練讀者的理解、推敲和聯想等多種閱讀技能。

寫作練習尤具新意，教讀者使用網式圖示（spidergrams）記錄重點，採用問答、書信、電報、記者採訪等多樣化形式，鼓勵讀者動手寫作。

書後更設有升級測試（Exit Test）及答案，供讀者檢查學習效果。充分利用書中的練習和測試，可全面提升聽、說、讀、寫四項技能。

④ 本系列還能提供甚麼幫助？

《Black Cat 優質英語階梯閱讀》提倡豐富多元的現代閱讀，巧用書中提供的資訊，有助於提升英語理解力，擴闊視野。

每本書都設有專章介紹相關的歷史文化知識，經典名著更有作者生平、社會背景等資訊。書內富有表現力的彩色插圖、繪圖和照片，使閱讀充滿趣味，部分加上如何解讀古典名畫的指導，增長見識。有的書還提供一些與主題相關的網址，比如關於不同國家的節慶源流的網址，讓讀者多利用網上資源增進知識。

CONTENTS

The first four chapters are recorded on the CD. 故事選錄

 These symbols indicate the beginning and end of the extracts
linked to the listening activities. 聽力練習開始和結束的標記

Daniel Defoe and his World

D aniel Defoe was born in London in the autumn of 1660.
No one knows his exact date of birth because his father
refused to register [1] his son's birth. Daniel was born into a
pre-industrial world, one in which there were no machines, no daily
newspapers and no rapid means of transportation or communication.
He was the son of James and Alice Foe. His father was a butcher
and an earnest, [2] devoted Puritan, [3] or Dissenter, as they were called
at that time.

Daniel was brought up in a family in which the predominant values

1. **register** : formally record something in a list.
2. **earnest** : very serious.
3. **Puritan** : member of a Protestant religious group in the 16th and 17th
   centuries.

were respectability, honesty, discipline, orderliness and self-sufficiency. One had to improve one's lot [1] through hard work.
When he was still a small boy his life was touched by two horrible events which he was to remember all his life: the Plague (1665) and the Great Fire of London (1666). During the Plague the mortality rate [2] was so high that many people, including the Defoes, fled to the countryside. Religious families like the Defoes considered the Plague a punishment sent by God for sinful [3] behaviour. Years later Defoe's memories of that period helped him to write *A Journal of the Plague Year.*

Burning the plague victims at night.

1. **lot** : the work or social position that you have.
2. **mortality rate** : death rate.
3. **sinful** : morally wrong.

The Great Fire of London quickly followed the Plague. It burned the city for four days and nights destroying St Paul's Cathedral, 87 parish churches, 13,000 houses and other important buildings. Young Daniel never forgot the city burning at night and the suffering of those who had lost everything.

When Daniel was 11 years old he was sent to boarding school in Dorking, Surrey for five years, where he studied Latin, Greek and English grammar.

In 1676 his father enrolled him at Reverend Charles Morton's dissenting academy, since he wanted his son to become a minister. Although Daniel Defoe never became a minister, he received an excellent education. Reverend Morton was an erudite [1] man and an

The Great Fire of London.

1. **erudite** : scholarly.

11

exceptional teacher. He taught his students to write in a clear, fluent style, to read the great works of literature and to think for themselves. Daniel was deeply influenced by Morton's teachings all his life.

The Old Custom House on the Thames;
one of the ports where English ships loaded and unloaded goods.

Trade had always attracted Daniel and in 1680 he became a London merchant, trading in wines and spirits, tobacco and other commodities. ¹ He worked in a pre-industrial society that was beginning to expand rapidly, particularly with overseas trade. During this period Daniel travelled extensively throughout England, Scotland and Europe.

He married Mary Tulfley in 1684 and they had eight children, two of whom died in infancy. Mary proved to be a loyal and patient wife.

In 1688 the forces of William of Orange landed at Torbay in Devon and invaded England without a fight. The Catholic King James II and his regime collapsed. The changes that took place in 1688-89 became known as 'The Glorious Revolution', which marked the end of the divine right of kings and the establishment of the supremacy of Parliament. Daniel Defoe was an enthusiastic supporter of 'The Glorious Revolution' and of the monarchs William and Mary. Daniel's business prospered for some years and he began to invest in risky ventures ² that led him to bankruptcy in 1692. The effect of bankruptcy on him and his family was devastating. ³

William of Orange.

1. **commodities** : products.
2. **ventures** : new business activities.
3. **devastating** : very destructive.

By 1705 he was able to pay a part of his debts, but he would never again be the London merchant he had been prior to [1] his bankruptcy. From the end of the century he became more and more interested in journalism and literary work, and began publishing political

Covent Garden Market (c. 1726).

1. **prior to** : before.

pamphlets. His pamphlet, *The Shortest Way with the Dissenters*, which attacked the State Church, caused his imprisonment for six months. During the years that followed (1704-13) he published his political newspaper, *The Review*, which was widely read and discussed in London. He was a talented and prolific [1] writer.

In 1719 he published his great work, *Robinson Crusoe*, a tale of adventure which was so successful with the newly-literate artisans and workmen that it was reprinted several times. The scholars of his epoch [2] considered his work 'non-serious' because it was fiction! Within four months of its publication it was followed by *The*

An early illustration for *Robinson Crusoe*.

Frontispiece to the first edition of *Robinson Crusoe*.

1. **prolific** : (here) producing many books.
2. **epoch** : a period of time in history.

Farther Adventures of Robinson Crusoe.
In 1720 he published *Captain Singleton*,
the story about a captain who turned into a
pirate. *Moll Flanders*, the autobiography [1]
of a prostitute, followed in 1722. His last
work was *Roxana* (1724), the
autobiography of a courtesan. [2]
Daniel Defoe, who created the English
novel as we know it today, died alone in
April 1731 at a lodging-house in
Ropemakers Alley, London, where he had
been hiding from one of his creditors.

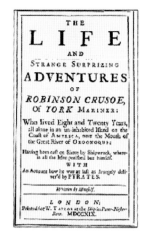

Title-page of the first
edition of *Robinson Crusoe*.

1 **Choose the correct answers.**

a. Daniel Defoe was born in London in the

- [ ] autumn of 1600.
- [ ] summer of 1606.
- [ ] autumn of 1660.

b. His father, James Foe,

- [ ] died during the terrible Plague.
- [ ] was a Puritan, or Dissenter.
- [ ] was very wealthy.

c. Religious families of Defoe's time

- [ ] believed in astrology.
- [ ] were not afraid of the Plague.
- [ ] considered the Plague a punishment sent by God.

1. **autobiography** : the story of
your life written by yourself.

2. **courtesan** : prostitute with
wealthy clients in former times.

d. Reverend Charles Morton's teachings
- ☐ inspired Defoe to become a minister.
- ☐ deeply influenced Defoe all his life.
- ☐ helped Defoe to become a rich merchant.

e. After becoming a London merchant, Daniel Defoe
- ☐ travelled to North America.
- ☐ travelled throughout England, Scotland and Europe.
- ☐ moved to Surrey with his family.

f. Defoe enthusiastically supported 'The Glorious Revolution' and
- ☐ the monarchs William and Mary.
- ☐ was injured during a battle of the revolution.
- ☐ wrote a pamphlet about it.

g. His risky investments
- ☐ made him a very rich man.
- ☐ led him to bankruptcy in 1692.
- ☐ were severely criticised by his wife.

h. Defoe's growing interest in journalism and literary work led him
- ☐ to sell his trading business.
- ☐ to debt and bankruptcy.
- ☐ to publish his political newspaper, *The Review*.

i. *Robinson Crusoe* (1719) was immensely successful with the newly-literate artisans and workmen,
- ☐ and also with the scholars of that time.
- ☐ but not with the scholars of his epoch.
- ☐ but it was never reprinted.

j. Today Daniel Defoe can justly be considered
- ☐ a great trader and merchant.
- ☐ the creator of political pamphlets.
- ☐ the creator of the English novel as we know it today.

Before reading

1 **Discuss the following with your friends.**

    a. What do you already know about Robinson Crusoe?

    b. Have you ever seen any films about him?

    c. Tell your friends what you already know.

2 **Listen to the first part of Chapter One and complete the following chart about Robinson.**

Date of birth	
Place of birth	
Family conditions	
His father's profession	
Robinson's original surname	
What happened to one brother	
What happened to the other brother	
Robinson's wish about the future	

Check your answers by reading the text.

CHAPTER ONE

ROBINSON'S ADVENTURES AT SEA

was born in the year 1632, in the city of York in England. My father was of a good family. He was a merchant from Bremen in Germany. He settled in England and made his fortune in trade, then he married. My mother's family name was Robinson. I was baptised Robinson Kreutznaer. However, in England we were always called Crusoe, so my friends call me Robinson Crusoe.

I had two brothers. One became a soldier and was killed in a battle against the Spaniards. I do not know what happened to my other brother. My father hoped I would study law, but I wanted to

go to sea. Although my mother and father did not want me to go, my desire was so strong that I ignored their wishes.

My father was a wise and serious man. He said that if I stayed at home my life would be easy and pleasant. Only desperate [1] men or very fortunate men went abroad, he said. I was neither desperate nor very fortunate. Mine was the middle state, [2] and he thought that the middle state was the best. The poor had a difficult life, and the rich were hated by the poor, said he. In the middle state a man could be happy. Kings often regretted [3] that they were not born in the middle state, and wise men prayed to have neither poverty nor wealth. He said that the greatest misfortunes in life were suffered by the rich and the poor. Only the man in the middle state can live in peace. He said that moderation, quietness, and good health were the conditions of the middle state.

He begged me not to abandon this happy condition. He told me that he had begged my brother not to become a soldier for the same reasons. However, my brother had run away to the army, and now he was dead. He said that God would not bless me if I went to sea, and that I would be sorry I had ignored my father's advice.

During the last part of his discourse [4] the tears ran down his face, especially when he spoke of my brother. When he said that I would

---

1. **desperate** : hopeless and ready to do anything.
2. **middle state** : neither rich nor poor.
3. **regretted** : were sorry (past tense of the verb 'to regret').
4. **discourse** : a serious speech.

Robinson's Adventures at Sea

regret my choice, he was so moved [1] that he could say no more.

I was sincerely affected by his words and decided not to think of going abroad any more. But alas! In a few days I began to dream of the sea again. I spoke to my mother. I told her that I still desired to go to sea and that nothing else would make me happy. I said that I was eighteen years old, too old to begin another profession. I asked her to persuade my father to let me go to sea.

This made her very angry. She said that it would be useless to speak to my father. If I wanted to ruin myself, she said, there was nothing she or my father could do to stop me. However, they would never agree to it.

A year later, I ran off to sea. This is how it happened. One day I went to the port of Hull. A friend of mine was going by sea to London in his father's ship. He asked me to go with him. Since it would cost me nothing, I decided to go, without even telling my mother and father. Thus on the first of September 1651 I went on board a ship for the first time.

---

1. **moved** : affected with emotion (past tense of the verb 'to move').

ROBINSON'S ADVENTURES AT SEA

As soon as the ship was at sea, the wind began to blow. I felt very sick and frightened. I thought that God was punishing me for leaving my father's house. The storm grew worse, although it was not as bad as many I have seen since. It was not even as bad as the storm I saw just a few days later, but it frightened me then. I thought the sea would swallow [1] us. I

---

1. **swallow** : cause something to disappear.

Robinson Crusoe

swore [1] to God that, if I lived, I would return to my father's house and never go to sea again.

The next day the sea grew calm and the sun shone. I no longer felt sick or frightened. My friend said, 'Well, Bob, how do you feel? Were you afraid?'

'It was a terrible storm,' said I.

'Do you call that a storm?' said he. 'That was nothing. Let's drink some rum and forget about it.'

We drank the rum, and I forgot my promise to God. A few days later, there was a really terrible storm. The waves were as high as mountains. I was very frightened. I felt sorry that I had forgotten my promise to God.

The sailors began to cry out that the ship would founder. [2] Fortunately, I did not know what the word 'founder' meant. I saw the captain and some others praying to God. At last we were rescued [3] by a boat from another ship. As we escaped, we saw our own ship go down. It was only then that I understood the word 'founder'.

When we reached the shore, the people were very kind to us. They gave us money to return to Hull or continue to London, as we pleased. If I had returned home, I would have been happy. My father, like the father in Christ's story of the

---

1. **swore** : promised solemnly with an oath (to swear - swore - sworn).
2. **founder** : sink.
3. **rescued** : saved.

prodigal [1] son, would have welcomed me. But I was foolish, and I did not go home.

The captain, who was my friend's father, said to me, 'Young man, you should never go to sea again.'

'Why, sir?' said I. 'Will you never go to sea again?'

'That is different,' said the captain. 'The sea is my profession. It is my duty to go to sea, but you made this voyage to see if you liked it. God has shown you that the sea is not for you. Perhaps that is why my ship foundered. You are like Jonah of the Bible story. I am sorry I ever allowed you on my ship!'

I went to London by land. How unwise young people are! They are not afraid to sin, [2] but they are afraid to seem foolish! I signed up [3] for a voyage to Africa. I should have signed up as a sailor. I could have learned the sailor's profession. In time, I might even have become a captain. However, I always made the worst choice, and I chose to go to sea as a gentleman. Therefore I had no duties on the ship, and I had no chance of learning to be a sailor.

I met the captain of a ship that had been on the coast of Africa. He had made good profits from the voyage and was eager to go again. He asked me to go with him as his companion. He said that I need not pay for the voyage. If I had any money, he said, he would show me how to make a profit in trade.

I accepted the offer, and became friends with the captain, who

---

1. **prodigal** : tending to waste money.
2. **sin** : break a religious or moral law.
3. **signed up** : enrolled, enlisted (past tense of the verb 'to sign up').

was a good and honest man. Following the captain's advice, I spent about forty pounds on things of little value. These I could trade for gold on the coast of Africa.

The voyage was a great success for me. Indeed, it was my only successful voyage. My friend the captain taught me the skills of both a sailor and a merchant. I brought home five pounds nine ounces [1] of gold, which I sold in London for nearly three hundred pounds.

Soon after our return to England, my friend died. I decided to do the same voyage again and signed up on the same ship with its new captain. As we approached the coast of Africa, we were pursued [2]

by a Turkish ship. After a short battle, the Turkish ship was victorious, and we were all taken as prisoners to the port of Sallee.

The captain of the Turkish ship made me his slave. I was horrified by this surprising change from merchant to miserable slave. I remembered my father's prophesy [3] that I would be miserable, and I realised that it had indeed been fulfilled. [4]

After about two years of slavery, I saw my chance of escape. One

---

1. **five pounds nine ounces** : about 2.5 kilos.
2. **pursued** : followed, chased (past tense of the verb 'to pursue').
3. **prophesy** : using religious or magical knowledge to say what will happen in the future.
4. **fulfilled** : (here) what his father had said really happened.

day, my master sent me out fishing with his brother Ismael and a black slave boy called Xury. The fishing boat was full of food, guns, and fresh water. While we were fishing, I pushed Ismael into the sea. He cried for help. I pointed a gun at him and said, 'I will not hurt you, if you do as I say. You swim well enough to reach the shore. [1] Go! Swim to the shore and leave us alone. If you do not, I will shoot you in the head, for I want my liberty.' [2]

Ismael swam away from the ship, and I turned to the slave boy. 'Xury,' said I, 'if you will be faithful [3] to me, I will make you a great man. If not, I will throw you into the sea too.' The boy smiled and promised to be faithful to me.

We sailed along the coast of Africa, close to the shore. Sometimes we heard lions and other wild beasts. We needed fresh water, but we were afraid to go ashore, for fear of wild beasts and savages. [4] Xury said that he would go ashore to get water, and I should wait in the boat.

'Why should you go, Xury?' I asked. 'Why should I not go, and you wait in the boat?'

Xury replied in words that made me love him ever after: 'If wild men come, they will eat me, and you will escape.'

'Well, Xury,' I said, 'we will both go. If wild men come we will kill them, and they will eat neither of us.' We went ashore and got fresh

---

1. **shore** : beach.
2. **liberty** : freedom.
3. **faithful** : loyal.
4. **savages** : people whose way of life is simple and primitive.

water. As we were returning to the boat, we saw a lion on the beach.

I aimed my gun and shot. Xury and I took the skin off the lion, for I thought it might be of some value. We sailed along the coast for ten days. I hoped that we would meet a European trading ship and be saved, but we did not meet one.

Sometimes we saw people on the shore. Their skin was black, and they were naked. [1] Once I thought of going ashore to meet them, but Xury advised against it. I made signs to them that we needed food. They brought meat and grain and left it on the beach for us. I made signs to thank them but had nothing to give them in payment.

However, we soon had the chance to do them a great service. Just as we reached our boat, a leopard [2] came running down from the mountain towards the beach. I shot it dead. The Negroes [3] were

1. **naked** : not wearing clothes.
2. **leopard** : a big wild cat which has yellow fur with black spots on it.
3. **Negroes** : in the 17th, 18th and 19th centuries, this word was used to indicate a black person. Today this word is no longer used and is considered derogatory, offensive and extremely rude.

amazed [1] and terrified by the sound of my gun. When they saw that the leopard was dead, they approached him. They wished to eat the flesh [2] of this animal. I made signs to tell them that they could have him, and they began cutting him up. They cut off his skin and gave it to me.

Leaving my friendly Negroes, I sailed on for eleven days. As we approached Cape Verde, Xury cried out, 'Master! A ship!' I saw that it was a Portuguese ship. I sailed towards it, and in three hours I reached it.

The men on the ship asked who I was. When I told them my story, they were very kind. They took me on board their ship with all my property [3] from the boat. I offered all my property to the captain, to thank him for saving

1. **amazed** : very surprised, astonished.
2. **flesh** : meat.
3. **property** : belongings.

me, but he would not take it. He said they were sailing to Brazil. He said that my property would be returned to me when we arrived. He offered to buy my boat from me. He paid me eighty pieces of eight [1] for it. He also offered me sixty pieces of eight for my boy Xury. I did not want to sell the poor boy's liberty because he had helped me to escape from slavery. Then the captain offered to set Xury free in ten years if he became a Christian. Xury said he was willing to go with him, so I let the captain have him.

About twenty-two days later we landed in All Saints' Bay in Brazil. I will never forget the captain's kindness. He bought a lot of my property from the boat. I left the ship with about two hundred and twenty pieces of eight.

In Brazil I saw how well the sugar planters [2] lived. They grew rich quickly. I decided to settle in Brazil and become a sugar planter. The first two years were difficult, but then my plantation grew prosperous. I was sorry that I had sold my boy Xury, for I needed help.

I was not happy in my new life. This was the middle state of which my father had spoken. I often said to myself, 'I could have done this at home, instead of coming five thousand miles to do it among strangers and savages.'

I thought I was like a man stranded alone [3] upon an island.

---

1. **pieces of eight** : gold coins.
2. **sugar planters** : owners of a plantation growing plants to produce sugar.
3. **stranded alone** : left helpless, abandoned in an isolated place.

Robinson's Adventures at Sea

Never compare your situation to a worse one! God may place you in the worse situation, so that you long for your old life! I say, God was just to leave me on an island, where I really was alone! If I had been content [1] to stay as I was, I would have been rich and happy. By leaving me on an island, God made me understand this.

The captain of the Portuguese ship advised me to send for some money. I had left my money with a friend in London. My friend sent me the money in the form of English goods. When they arrived, I thought that my fortune was made. I sold the goods at a great profit for about four hundred pounds. As soon as I got this money, I bought myself a Negro slave.

After four years, I had learned the language and made some friends among my fellow planters. I told them of the trade in Negro slaves on the African coast. 'If a merchant takes knives, hatchets, [2] and other things of little value,' I said, 'he can easily trade them for gold and Negro slaves.'

They listened very attentively, especially to the part about buying slaves. There were very few slaves in Brazil at the time, and they cost a lot of money. Three planters came to me the next morning. They said they planned to buy a ship and sail to the African coast to buy slaves. They wanted to make one voyage only, then share [3] the slaves among their plantations. [4] They asked me if I would go on this voyage, and they promised that I would have a share of slaves without spending any money.

---

1. **content** : happy and satisfied.
2. **hatchets** :
3. **share** : divide, distribute.
4. **plantations** : large farms.

Robinson Crusoe

I agreed to go. I went aboard the ship on the first of September 1659, exactly eight years after my first voyage from Hull. We sailed up the coast to Cape St Augustino, then we lost sight of [1] land. Twelve days later, a hurricane [2] hit our ship. For twelve days the winds blew strongly. Every day I expected the sea to swallow us.

On the twelfth day, the weather was a little calmer. The ship was filling with water, so I advised the captain to sail for Barbados. As we sailed another storm hit us. The wind blew us far away from the trading routes. If we came to land, we would probably be eaten by savages.

One morning, a sailor cried out, 'Land!' We ran out to look, but at that moment the ship struck [3] sand. The waves broke over the ship, and we thought we would all die.

We could not move the ship off the sand. We were sure that the ship would soon break into pieces. Therefore, we climbed into a boat and left the ship. We rowed through that wild water towards the land, knowing that we were rowing towards our greatest danger. Then a great wave came and the boat turned over.

Though I was a good swimmer, I could not get my breath [4] in this stormy sea. A wave carried me along towards the shore. It left me on the sand, half-drowned. I stood up and walked fast towards the beach. I knew another wave would soon break over me. The sea

---

1. **lost sight of...** : didn't see any more (past tense of the verb 'to lose sight').
2. **hurricane** : a violent storm.
3. **struck** : hit (to strike - struck - struck).
4. **get my breath** : be able to breathe comfortably.

rose behind me like a mountain. I held my breath, and the wave carried me closer to the shore. I tried to stand up and get my breath again, but another wave broke over me. I was carried with great force and speed towards the shore. Then my head shot [1] above the water, and I was able to breathe for a moment. I was covered with water again, then that wave too began to withdraw. [2]

I felt the earth under my feet. I ran towards the shore, but twice more the waves came over me. The last time nearly killed me. The sea threw me hard against a rock. I held on to the rock as the next wave broke over me. When the wave withdrew, I ran to the beach, climbed over the rocks, and lay down on the grass.

1. **shot** : moved quickly and suddenly (to shoot - shot - shot).
2. **withdraw** : move back (to withdraw - withdrew - withdrawn).

1 Use the words in the box below to complete the following sentences.

> suggestions   greatest   peace   lucky   sea
> conditions   middle-state   quietness   be
> wished   happy   remained   follow   rich
> poor   life   desperate

a. If Robinson .... at home, his .... would be pleasant.

b. Only .... men or .... men went abroad.

c. The .... was the best because a man could be .... and live in ....

d. Wise men .... to be neither .... nor rich.

e. The .... and the poor suffered the .... misfortunes.

f. Moderation, ... and good health were the .... of the middle state.

g. If Robinson went to ...., God would not bless him.

h. Robinson would .... sorry if he did not .... his father's ....

2 Tick the correct answers following these statements:

a. Robinson decided not to think of going abroad because
- [ ] he was moved by his father's words.
- [ ] he had spoken to his mother.
- [ ] he desired to stay at home.

b. Robinson asked his mother to
- [ ] help him to start a new profession.
- [ ] make him happy.
- [ ] persuade his father to allow him to go to sea.

c. Robinson's mother was very
- [ ] happy.
- [ ] indifferent.
- [ ] angry.

d. Robinson went to sea
- [ ] after two years.
- [ ] after one month.
- [ ] one year later.

e. Robinson was asked to leave on a ship by
- [ ] a friend of his.
- [ ] a friend of his father's.
- [ ] his own father.

f. While the ship was at sea there
- [ ] was a storm.
- [ ] were two storms on different days.
- [ ] was good weather.

g. During the storms Robinson felt
- [ ] excited.
- [ ] happy.
- [ ] scared.

h. Then
- [ ] the ship sank.
- [ ] the sea grew calm.
- [ ] Robinson prayed to God.

i. On the shore Robinson and the crew received
- [ ] food.
- [ ] shelter.
- [ ] money.

j. The captain warned Robinson
- [ ] not to go to sea again.
- [ ] not to return home.
- [ ] to pray to God.

k. In London Robinson signed up for a voyage to Africa as a
- [ ] sailor.
- [ ] captain.
- [ ] gentleman.

3 Listen to the section of the text on pages 25-26. Then number the following events which are given in scrambled order to reconstruct what happened to Robinson.

- [ ] Robinson did not need to pay for the voyage.
- [ ] Robinson spent about forty pounds on things of little value which he would exchange for gold in Africa.
- [ ] Robinson sold his gold in London.
- [ ] Robinson met the captain of a ship that had been on the coast of Africa.
- [ ] Robinson learnt how to be a good sailor and merchant.

☐ The captain and Robinson became friends.

☐ After his return to England, Robinson decided to do the same voyage again.

☐ Robinson and the crew were made prisoners and taken to the port of Sallee.

☐ The ship on which Robinson was travelling was attacked by the Turks.

☐ Robinson was made a slave.

Read the text again and check your answers.

4 **Look at the map and use arrows to reconstruct Robinson's voyage. Then answer the following questions:**

a. Where was Robinson born?

b. Where did he start his first voyage from?

c. What happened during the voyage?

d. Where did Robinson go after the ship had sunk?

e. What happened in London?

f. Was the voyage to Africa successful?

g. What happened during the second voyage to Africa?

h. To which port was Robinson taken?

i. What happened to him later?

j. How and when did he escape?

5 Complete the following table.

Place where they landed	....
What Robinson decided to be	....
Why Robinson regretted selling Xury	....
What the captain of the Portuguese ship suggested to him	....
In which form Robinson got the money	....
What Robinson did with the money he got by selling the goods	....
How long Robinson took to learn the language	....
Main problem about slaves in Brazil	....
What the planters asked Robinson to do	....

6 Look again at pages 32-33 and write suitable questions for the following answers:

a. When ....? On the first of September 1659.

b. When ....? Twelve days later.

c. What ....? A little calmer.

d. What ....? Another storm hit them.

e. Why ....? Because a great wave came.

f. What ....? A wave.

g. Where ....? On the grass.

Summary

Fill in the missing words. The first letter of each word has been given to help you.

Robinson Crusoe w............ b............ in York in 1632. His greatest
d............ was to go to s............, so, when he was n............ he ran
off to the port of H............ . During the voyage there were two
s............ and the second one caused the ship to s............ .
However, Robinson and the crew were r............ by a boat.
Robinson then s............ u............ for a voyage to Africa and
learned how to be a good s............ and m............ . He signed up
for another v............ to Africa but this time the ship was p............
by Turks and they were made p............ and taken to the port of
Sallee. After two years of s............ he managed to e............ in a
boat with Xury, a black slave boy. After eleven days they a............
Cape Verde where a P............ ship rescued them. The captain took
Robinson to B............ and Robinson s............ Xury to him. In
Brazil Robinson became a s............ p............ and was p............ .
After four years three planters asked him to go on a voyage with
them to b............ slaves in Africa. They l............ on the first of
S............ 1659 but twelve days later there was a great storm and
the boat t............ o............ . Robinson managed to s............ to
land.

The Slave Trade

In Chapter One Robinson became a slave and later, when he was a free man, he bought a slave. On page 31 Robinson explained nonchalantly [1] to his friends that black slaves could easily be bought on the African coast.

During this period of history, slaves and in particular black slaves, were considered a commodity which could be easily bought and sold at slave markets. The slave trade became a huge, lucrative [2] business which did not take into account the immense [3] suffering and humiliation of these poor human beings.

The English, French and Portuguese had traded in slaves since the middle of the 16th century. Sir John Hawkins, one of Queen Elizabeth's privateers, became the first Englishman to trade in

Sir John Hawkins.

Sir John Hawkins was the captain of *The Jesus of Lübeck*.

1. **nonchalantly** : casually.
2. **lucrative** : profitable.
3. **immense** : great.

African slaves. English sea captains traded cloth, guns and cheap iron goods for West African slaves captured by local slave traders. These wretched [1] people were brutally [2] captured, crammed into ships and chained to the lower decks for their entire journey across the Atlantic Ocean. From the 1500s to the 1800s, about 12 million Africans were shipped across the Atlantic. Some of the slaves did not survive the ordeal. [3] About two million died during the journey. Those who survived were sold to tobacco and sugar plantation owners, mainly in Jamaica and Barbados, where they worked incredibly long hours in a very hot climate. Their living conditions were appalling. [4]

The captains of the slave ships made a handsome profit with the

African slaves on a slave ship.

1. **wretched** : miserable or pitiable.
2. **brutally** : cruelly.
3. **ordeal** : painful experience.
4. **appalling** : extremely bad.

profit with the slave trade. Before returning home from Jamaica or Barbados, their ships were loaded with tobacco and sugar products which were sold for an even greater profit in England!

Great Britain had set up colonies on the east coast of mainland America during the first part of the 17th century. The New England colonies engaged in [1] a 'triangular slave trade', which involved slaves, sugar cane and rum. Sugar cane was brought from the West Indies to New England where

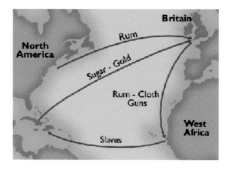

The 'Triangular Slave Trade'.

A 'blackbirder' and his human cargo in the Pacific.

1. **engaged in** : took part in.

41

it was refined and made into rum. The rum was then traded on the West Coast of Africa for black slaves. The slaves who endured [1] the extenuating [2] journey across the Atlantic were sold to plantation owners in the West Indies.

Tobacco, cotton and sugar cane were the most important products of the British colonies of the south-eastern American mainland. They were cultivated by black slaves on huge plantations. These products

Slaves cutting sugar cane, 1860.

continued to be the backbone of the South's economy even after the American Revolution (1775-1781), when the thirteen colonies declared their independence from Great Britain and formed the United States of America. The misery and suffering of the plantation slaves inspired the American author, Harriet Beecher Stowe, to write the novel *Uncle Tom's Cabin*, a touching story that intensified [3] anti-slavery sentiment [4] in the North. Slavery in the South was one of the reasons that led to the American Civil War of 1861. In 1865 the South lost the war against the North and slavery was abolished [5] in the United States.

1. **endured** : suffered something painful.

2. **extenuating** : making wrongdoing less serious by giving an excuse.

3. **intensified** : caused something to become more serious.

4. **sentiment** : feelings.

5. **abolished** : (here) ended the existence of slavery.

1 Fill in the gaps with the words in the box.

> triangular   tobacco   lucrative   rum
> survived   colonies   sugar cane   plantation
> abolished   South   commodity   African slaves
> journey   east   cotton

a. During Robinson Crusoe's time slaves were considered a
....

b. The slave trade was a very .... business.

c. Sir John Hawkins was the first Englishman to trade in
....

d. The slaves that .... the terrible
.... across the Atlantic were sold to
.... owners.

e. Great Britain set up .... on the
.... coast of mainland America.

f. The New England '........................... slave trade' involved
slaves, ... and ....

g. ...., sugar cane and .... were the
backbone of the economy of the ....

h. After the American Civil War of 1861 slavery was
.... in the United States of America.

Before reading

1 If you were to live on a desert island for some time, what things would you want to have with you? (Remember you must think about survival!)

....
....
....
....
....

CHAPTER TWO

STRANDED ON THE ISLAND

I looked up and thanked God for saving my life. A short time before there had seemed to be no hope. It is impossible to describe the joy of someone who has just escaped death. I alone had survived; all my companions were dead. When I saw how far away the ship was, I was amazed that I had been able to get to the shore.

I then began to look around me, to see what kind of a place I was in. My joy left me. I was wet, I had no other clothes, and I had nothing to eat or drink. Surely I would die of starvation [1] or be eaten by wild animals. I had no gun with which to hunt for food or defend myself. For a while I ran around, trembling and

---

1. **starvation** : suffering or death caused by lack of food.

ROBINSON CRUSOE

crying. Night came. I walked around, looking for fresh water. When I found some, I drank, then I climbed up a tree to sleep.

When I awoke the sun was shining. The waves had moved the ship closer to the shore during the night. I realised that if we had stayed on board we would all have survived the storm. This thought made the tears run down my face.

I took off my clothes and swam to the ship. I climbed aboard and looked around. The ship's store [1] of food was not wet. I needed a boat or raft [2] to carry the goods back to the shore. There were several large pieces of wood on the ship. I threw them into the sea then jumped in myself and tied them all together with rope. In this way, after a lot of time and effort, I made a raft.

I then loaded the raft with food, clothes, tools, guns, and bullets, all packed in wooden boxes. I got onto the raft and returned to the shore. A short distance from where I had landed the night before, I saw a river. I landed the raft a little way up the river and got all my goods on the shore.

I did not yet know whether I was on the mainland or on an island. I took a gun and climbed a hill. From the top of the hill I saw that I was on an island. I saw many birds, but no animals or

---

1. **ship's store** : place on the ship where supplies of goods are kept.
2. **raft** : a sort of boat made of flat pieces of wood tied together.

people. On my way back down the hill, I shot a bird. I believe it was the first gun fired there since the creation of the world. At the sound, thousands of birds rose screaming [1] into the air.

That evening I set wooden boards [2] and boxes around me to protect me as I slept.

---

1. **screaming** : crying out.
2. **boards** : flat pieces of wood.

ROBINSON CRUSOE

The next day I returned to the ship. This time I got a hammock, [1] blankets, [2] hatchets, a perspective glass [3] and sails. [4]

Back on the shore, I made a tent out of one of the sails. I brought everything into the tent that could be ruined by rain or sun. Then I made a bed and slept in it quietly all night, for I was very tired from the work of the day.

I had the largest store, I believe, that was ever laid up for one man. However, I was not satisfied. The ship had not yet broken to pieces, and I thought I should get everything I could out of her. Every day I went to the ship and brought back more goods. I brought bread, rum, sugar, and many other things back to my tent.

Finally there was nothing more to take out of the ship. I then began to take pieces of the ship itself. Iron, nails, rope – I carried away everything I could.

I had now been on the island for thirteen days and had been eleven times on board the ship. I think that if the weather had remained calm I would have brought the whole ship away piece by piece.

The last time I went to the ship I found money. I smiled and said, 'Oh, drug! What are you good for? One knife is worth more [5]

---

1. **hammock** : netting canvas hung up by the corners and used as a bed.
2. **blankets** : covers for keeping warm.
3. **perspective glass** : a magnifying glass for looking at things in the distance; the equivalent of modern binoculars.
4. **sails** : sheets of strong cloth spread to catch the wind, by which a ship is driven forward.
5. **worth more** : more valuable.

Stranded on the Island

to me than all this money. I will leave you here! You are a creature whose life is not worth saving!' However, on second thoughts, I took it away.

Then clouds covered the sky and the wind began to blow. I went home to my tent, where I lay with all my wealth around me, very secure. There was a bad storm that night. In the morning the ship was gone.

END

I now began to think about protecting myself from savages and wild animals. I wanted to build my house in a place that was near a fresh water supply. It should be sheltered [1] from the sun. It should be safe from attack. Finally, it should face the sea, so that I could see any ship that came near the island. (I still hoped to be rescued).

I found a little flat shelf on the side of a hill. There was a cliff behind it, so that nothing could attack me from behind. In front, the hill descended [2] to the beach. It was on the north side of the hill, so that it was sheltered from the sun all day.

I built my tent against the cliff. Then I built a high, strong, wooden fence [3] in a semicircle around the front of my tent. I made a ladder. When I was inside, I could bring the ladder in after me. In this way neither man nor beast could enter my house.

It took a lot of time and effort to carry all my goods inside.

---

1. **sheltered** : protected.
2. **descended** : went down.
3. **fence** : line of wooden posts which are joined by wood or wire for protection.

ROBINSON CRUSOE

Then I began to dig out [1] a cave in the cliff behind my tent, because I needed a place to store my property. After a big storm, I was afraid that lightning might strike [2] my great box of gunpowder. [3] Therefore, I made many small boxes and put the gunpowder in them. These I hid in places secure from lightning.

Every day I went out hunting. There were goats [4] on the island. I shot a she-goat that had a little kid by her. This made me very sad. When I carried the dead she-goat to my house, the kid followed me, but it would not eat. I was therefore forced to kill it and eat it.

I thought about my situation a lot. The storm had blown the ship hundreds of miles away from the European trading routes. Therefore, I thought, it was God's will that I should spend the rest of my life on this miserable island. I often asked myself why God chose to ruin his creatures. It seemed hardly rational [5] to be thankful for such a life.

Then one day, when I was walking on the beach with my gun,

---

1. **dig out** : to turn up earth with a spade (to dig - dug - dug).
2. **strike** : hit.
3. **gunpowder** : explosive in the form of a powder.
4. **goats** : animals of the sheep family, with horns and long-haired coats.
5. **hardly rational** : almost not using reason.

ROBINSON CRUSOE

I thought, 'Certainly you are miserable, but what happened to the others? You alone were fortunate enough to survive. Is it better to be on this island or at the bottom of the sea?'

Then I thought how well-equipped I was to survive on the island. What would have happened to me if the ship had not been blown closer to shore? That happy chance allowed me to take all these things from the ship. How would I have lived without guns and bullets, tools, and clothes?

I was afraid that I would forget what day it was. I might even forget the Sabbath. [1] Therefore, I planted a great wooden cross on the beach, and on it I carved [2] these words with my knife: 'I came on shore here on the 30 of September 1659'. Upon the sides of the post I made a small cut with my knife every day, a longer cut every Sunday, and an even longer cut for the first day of every month.

I forgot to say before that among the things I took from the ship were some Catholic prayer books and three Bibles. There were also two cats and a dog on board the ship. I carried the cats back with me to the island. The dog jumped into the sea and swam after me.

I tried to comfort myself by listing the comforts I enjoyed beside the miseries I suffered like this:

---

1. **Sabbath** : the day of the week intended for rest and worship of God; Saturday for Jewish people and Sunday for Christians.
2. **carved** : cut into wood (past tense of the verb 'to carve').

STRANDED ON THE ISLAND

Evil	Good
I am stranded on an island, with no hope of being saved.	But I am alive, not drowned as were the other men on the ship.
I have been singled out. [1] I alone am chosen to lead this miserable life.	But I have also been singled out to survive, and He who saved me can deliver [3] me from this condition.
I am separated from mankind, without human society.	But I am not starving. There is food on the island.
I have no clothes to cover me.	But the weather is hot, and I do not need clothes.
I have no means of defending myself against attack by man or beast.	But I see no wild beasts on this island. What if I had been shipwrecked on the coast of Africa, where I saw the lion and the leopard?
I have no soul [2] to speak to.	But God sent the ship near enough to the shore that I have been able to supply [4] myself with many things.

This showed me clearly that even in the most miserable conditions there are things for which to be thankful.

---

1. **singled out** : specifically chosen.
2. **soul** : person.
3. **deliver** : save.
4. **supply** : provide.

ROBINSON CRUSOE

🎧 Robinson Crusoe's Journal [1]

September 30, 1659. I, poor miserable Robinson Crusoe, was shipwrecked near the shore of this unfortunate island, which I call the Island of Despair.

October 1 to October 24. I spent my time getting all I could out of the ship. It often rained during these days, this being the rainy season.

October 25. It rained all day and night. The bad weather broke the ship into pieces. I spent this day hiding my goods from the rain.

October 26 to October 30. I found a place in which to build my house and worked very hard carrying all my property to this place.

October 31. I went out with my gun to find food. I shot a she-goat.

November 1. I set up my tent and my hammock.

November 2. I set wooden boxes and boards to form a fence around my tent.

November 3. I went out with my gun and killed two birds, which were very good food. In the afternoon I began to make myself a table.

November 4. This morning I began to plan my time. Every morning after this I walked out with my gun for two or three hours if it did not rain. I worked until about eleven o'clock, then I ate. From twelve to two, when it was very hot, I slept. In the evening I worked again.

---

1. **journal** : a written record.

Stranded on the Island

November 5. This day I went out with my gun and my dog. I killed a wild cat. Her skin was soft, but I could not eat the meat. I skinned [1] every creature that I killed and kept the skin.

November 6. I finished my table but was not satisfied with it.

November 7. Now the weather began to be pleasant. From the seventh to the twelfth I worked at making myself a chair (except for the eleventh, which was a Sunday). I was not satisfied with the chair.

---

1. **skinned** : removed the skin (past tense of the verb 'to skin').

ROBINSON CRUSOE

Note: I soon forgot which days were Sundays, having forgotten to make the longer cut on the post.

November 13. This day it rained, which cooled the earth and refreshed me. There was terrible thunder and lightning. I decided to separate my powder into many small boxes and to store them far from each other.

November 14, 15, and 16. I spent these three days making little boxes for my powder. On one of these days I killed a large bird that was good to eat, but I do not know its name.

November 17. This day I began to dig in the rock behind my tent to make a cave in which to store my goods.
Note: I needed two things for this work – a pick-axe [1] and a shovel. [2] I stopped my work to make these tools. I made a pick-axe out of the pieces of iron I had taken from the ship, but I had no idea how to make a shovel.   END

November 18. In the woods I found an iron tree, so called because its wood is very hard. With great difficulty, I cut a piece of this wood, carried it home, and carved it into the form of a shovel. The making of these tools took me four days.

November 23. I began work on the cave again and worked for eighteen days. At the end of that time, the cave was large enough to hold all my goods.

---

1. **pick-axe** :
2. **shovel** : tool like a spade, with a short handle.

$TRANDED ON THE I$LAND

December 10. Just when I had finished my cave, the roof fell in. This frightened me. If I had been inside at the time I would have been killed. I carried out all the fallen earth and built props [1] to hold up the roof so that it would not fall down again.

December 17. From this day to the twenty-seventh, I built shelves.

December 20. I carried all my property into the cave and put everything in order.

December 24. It rained all day and night, so that I could not go out.

December 25. Rain all day.

December 26. No rain. The earth was much cooler than before.

December 27. I killed a young goat and shot another in the leg. I led the wounded [2] goat home and took care of it. It lived and grew tame. [3] It ate the grass around my house and would not go away. This gave me the idea of breeding the goats so that they would grow up tame and provide me with food when my gunpowder was finished.

January 3 to April 14. I built a fence around my house. I cut branches [4] from trees and planted them deep in the ground. After a while, they began to grow, so that my fence looked like a natural thing.

---

1. **props** : supports.
2. **wounded** : injured.
3. **tame** : not wild or dangerous.
4. **branches** : arm-like parts of a tree.

1 Listen to the first part of Chapter Two and decide whether the following statements are true (T) or false (F). Put crosses in the right column:

	T	F
a. Robinson thanked God for saving his life.	☐	☐
b. Robinson was the only survivor.	☐	☐
c. Robinson had a gun.	☐	☐
d. Robinson slept on the grass.	☐	☐
e. When Robinson awoke it was foggy.	☐	☐
f. The ship's food-store was dry.	☐	☐
g. Robinson made a big boat.	☐	☐
h. Going up the hill Robinson realised he was on an island.	☐	☐
i. Robinson collected some more things from the boat the next day.	☐	☐
j. Robinson made a hut.	☐	☐
k. Robinson left the money on the ship.	☐	☐
l. The ship was destroyed by a storm.	☐	☐

Read the text again and check your answers.
Correct the false statements.

2 You are Robinson Crusoe and you want to write a letter to your father telling him about your incredible adventure. You plan to put the letter in a bottle and throw it out to sea for someone to find.

3 Read pages 49-50, then complete:

    a. Robinson wanted to build a house because ....

    b. The house had to be built in front of the sea in order that ....

    c. Robinson found a .... on the side of the hill backed by a cliff so that ....

    d. Robinson built his .... against the cliff on the north side so that ....

    e. Then Robinson built a wooden .... around the tent to ....

    f. Robinson also made a .... in order to ....

    g. He dug out a cave behind his tent because ....

4 Complete the following tables.

Things that Robinson brought from the ship	Use Robinson made of them
eg.: hatchets	to make a fence, to cut wood...
....	....
....	....
....	....
....	....

Things that Robinson made for himself on the island	Use Robinson made of them
eg.: ladder	to climb over the fence...
....	....
....	....
....	....
....	....

5 Read pages 50 and 52 and discuss the following with your friends:

a. why Robinson felt miserable.

b. why Robinson felt fortunate.

c. what Robinson did to avoid forgetting what day it was.

d. what books Robinson had taken from the ship.

e. what animals Robinson had taken from the ship.

f. what Robinson did to comfort himself.

6 After reading the evil/good list on page 53, try to complete the following table.

Negative Aspects	Positive Aspects
he had no means of defending himself	but there were no...
	but the weather was hot
he had no soul to speak to	but he had been able...
	but he hoped God would save him
he was alone	
	but he was alive

7 Discuss the following with your friends.

– Whether a journal is:

a. a form of communication.

b. a daily record of events.

c. a daily record of thoughts.

d. a daily record of appointments.

e. a daily record of business transactions.

f. a daily record of news.

– Why you think that Robinson decided to keep a journal.

– What you would have done in the same situation.

8 Listen to the section of the text on pages 54-56 and number these sentences so as to put them in the right order. Two have been done for you.

☐1☐ Robinson was shipwrecked on an island which he called the Island of Despair on September 30, 1659.

☐ Robinson shot a she-goat.

☐ Robinson killed two birds.

☐ The bad weather broke the ship into pieces.

☐5☐ Robinson set up his tent and hammock.

☐ Robinson started to plan his time.

☐ Robinson made himself a chair.

☐ Robinson got all he could out of the ship.

☐ Robinson started to dig in the rock to make a cave.

☐ Robinson built a fence around his tent.

Check your answers by reading the text. In your notebook, summarise what Robinson did in your own words.

9 Vocabulary

Read the definitions and write the words.

a. A large hollow in a rock: ....

b. To put in a safe place for the future: ....

c. Made of wood: ....

d. To provide: ....

e. Suffering caused by lack of food: ....

f. Protected: ....

g. Explosive in the form of a powder: ....

Summary

Read the following summary and use the words in the box to fill in the gaps.

> hammock   knife   goats   ship
> fence   journal   tree   gunpowder
> cliff   hill   tent

Robinson thanked God for saving his life. The first night he slept in
a .... The following day he swam to the .... and
took food, clothes, tools, guns and bullets. Every day he returned to
the ship to take other things – a ...., blankets, hatchets, a
perspective glass and sails – until there was nothing more to take. To
protect himself from the savages and wild animals he decided to
build a .... on the north side of a .... Then he
built a .... around the house. Next he dug a cave in the
.... to store his .... Although he was miserable
he decided that it was God's wish that he was on the island and he
tried to comfort himself by listing the positive aspects of his
situation as well as the negative ones. He planted a big wooden cross
on the beach and made a small cut with his .... every day
to remember what day it was. He also started writing a ....
To provide himself with food he decided to breed ....

Shipwrecks!

Ever since man began navigating there have been shipwrecks. Most shipwrecks were caused by storms, tempests [1] and adverse [2] weather conditions. Writers and painters have always been fascinated by man's struggle with the elements – his victories and his defeats.

The floors of our seas and oceans are filled with shipwrecks of the

The Wreck of the Dutton at Plymouth, 26 January 1796
by Thomas Luny.

1. **tempests** : violent storms.   2. **adverse** : unfavourable.

past – Phoenician, Egyptian, Greek, Roman, Spanish, Portuguese, to name but a few. The *Titanic* is probably the most famous shipwreck of the 20th century.

Shipwrecks and pirate attacks were the two greatest dangers for seafaring [1] people of the past. These dangers added to the general overall physical hardships of life at sea: malnutrition, [2] scurvy, [3] illness, serious injuries and amputation of an arm or limb by the ship's 'surgeon'. The psychological hardships of being far from home, not being able to see land for months at a time and living in

The Shipwreck by Aivazoffkski.

1. **seafaring** : associated with travelling by sea.
2. **malnutrition** : bad health caused by a lack of food.
3. **scurvy** : an illness caused by a lack of vitamin C.

extremely crowded and often dirty living quarters, were detrimental [1]
to the crew's morale. [2]

Today shipwrecks have become a subject of study for marine
archaeologists who use sophisticated equipment to search for
treasures and artefacts [3] that enrich our knowledge of the past.

1 **Discuss the following with your friends.**

    a. What were the two greatest dangers at sea for seafaring people
of the past?

    b. Describe the physical and psychological hardships at sea.

    c. Who studies shipwrecks today?

    d. Look at the painting on page 64 and briefly describe what is
happening.

Titanic, by George Washington Sandell.

1. **detrimental** : harmful.
2. **morale** : the level of confidence and positive feelings among a group of
people.
3. **artefacts** : objects made by man which were historically important.

A   C   T   I   V   I   T   I   E   S

Before reading

1 **Listen to the first part of Chapter Three. Then answer the following questions.**

    a. What did Robinson find among his goods?

    ....

    b. What did he decide to store in it?

    ....

    c. What kinds of plants started growing?

    ....

    d. Why did Robinson think of God?

    ....

    e. Why did he carefully save the grain?

    ....

    f. What could Robinson do with the ladder?

    ....

    g. Why did Robinson think his cave was falling in?

    ....

    h. What had actually happened?

    ....

    i. How long did the storm last?

    ....

CHAPTER THREE

LORD OF THE ISLAND

ne day, I found among my goods a little bag that had once held grain on board our ship. I decided to use it to store my powder, so I shook it out near the rock outside my house. Soon afterwards the rains came. A month later, I saw some young plants growing there. I had forgotten all about the grain bag. When the plants grew, I was surprised to see that some were our English barley and others were rice.

Up to this point, I had very little idea of religion. I thought of everything that had happened to me as chance. When I saw English barley growing there, I thought it was a miracle. [1] God had made it grow there to comfort me.

---

1. **miracle** : an event that is impossible according to the ordinary laws of nature.

LORD OF THE ISLAND

This thought brought tears to my eyes. Then I remembered shaking out the bag in that place just before the rains came. This calmed my mind. I thought the grain had grown there by chance, and so I felt less thankful to God. But I should have been thankful anyway, because the chance of grain growing there was very small. By chance ten or twelve grains of barley and rice had remained in the bottom of the bag. By chance I had shaken out the bag in the shade of the rock, where it was protected from the sun. I carefully saved the grain to plant again, hoping to grow enough to supply me with bread.

April 16. I finished my ladder. With this I could climb over the fence. The fence was now thick and high. From outside, the house could not be seen. At last I was safe from attack by man or beast.

The next day, the earth came falling down from the roof of my cave and the hill above it. I thought that my cave was falling in as it had done before. I climbed the fence, for fear of being buried alive. Once outside, I realised that it was an earthquake. [1]

I was terrified that the hill would fall upon my tent and bury [2] all my goods. I sat on the ground, feeling miserable. The wind rose and there was a great storm. It lasted about three hours. All that time I sat on the ground, terrified and miserable, but I never had one serious religious thought.

END

Two hours later, the air and sea were calm, and it began to rain. I realised that the storm had been the result of the

---

1. **earthquake** : shaking of the earth's surface.
2. **bury** : put underground.

69

earthquake and that the earthquake was now over. I went in and sat in my tent.

June 16. On the beach at the other side of the island I found a large turtle. [1] I had never seen one before, but I soon discovered that there were many on the other side of the island.

June 19. I fell ill and began shivering. [2]

June 20. I did not sleep all night because of the fever.

June 21. I was terrified by my illness and had no one to help me. I prayed to God for the first time since the storm on the sea by Hull. I could not think clearly. For several days I lay shivering with fever.

June 26. I woke up feeling better. Having no food, I took my gun and killed a goat. I found it very difficult to carry the goat home, because I was weak from my illness.

---

1. **turtle** : a kind of large tortoise.
2. **shivering** : trembling, shaking.

LORD OF THE ISLAND

June 27. I fell ill again and lay in bed all day without food or drink. I tried to pray to God, but all I could say was 'Lord have mercy [1] upon me' over and over again. I fell asleep and had a terrible dream.

I dreamt I was sitting on the ground outside my house. I saw a man descend from the sky. He was clothed in fire and held a spear [2] in his hand. When he landed on the ground before me, the earth trembled. He moved towards me to kill me. Then he said, *'Since you do not repent, [3] now you will die.'*

I awoke terrified. Alas! I had no religious knowledge. What my father had taught me had all been forgotten in eight years of a wicked [4] sailor's life. My soul had been stupid. It had not desired good. It had not feared evil.

Through all my misfortunes I had never once thought that they were the just punishment for my sins. I had acted like an animal, guided by my passions. When the rice and barley grew, I had a moment of serious religious thought, but that passed when I discovered that it was not a miracle.

Now, for the first time, I began seriously to repent of my sinful life. I saw my condition not as simple misfortune but as the punishment of a just God. These thoughts brought tears to my eyes. I remembered my father's words. He had said that, if I went

---

1. **mercy** : pity.
2. **spear** :
3. **repent** : be sorry for something you have done.
4. **wicked** : bad, sinful.

to sea, God would not bless me and I would be sorry. 'Now,' I said to myself, 'my father's prophesy has really been fulfilled. God has punished me, and there is no one to help me.' Then I cried out, 'Lord help me, for I am in great distress!' [1]

June 28. Feeling a little stronger, I ate some turtle meat. This was the first time in my life I asked God's blessing on what I ate. Afterwards, I took my gun and walked to the shore. There I sat down, feeling weak once more, and looked out at the sea. 'What,' I asked myself, 'is this earth and sea of which I have seen so much? What am I? What are men and beasts? Where do we come from? Surely we are made by the same secret power that formed the earth and sea. Who is that?' The answer was clear: 'God made it all.' Then I thought, 'if God made all these things, He must also guide them all. Nothing can happen in creation without His knowledge. [2] Therefore, He knows that I am here in this miserable condition, and he meant these things to happen to me.'

'Why has God done this to me?' I asked myself. But then I remembered my wicked life, and I said to myself, 'Why do you ask why God has done this to you? Ask instead why you were not killed long ago'.

Sadly disturbed by these thoughts, I went to my chest [3] to look for some tobacco. There I also found the Bibles I had taken from

---

1. **distress** : sorrow and pain.
2. **knowledge** : (here) awareness.
3. **chest** : large wooden box.

LORD OF THE ISLAND

the ship. I took one of the Bibles and began to read. The first words I saw were these: *'Call on me in the day of trouble, and I will deliver [1] you, and you will praise me.'* The words were very relevant to my situation, and I often thought about them afterwards. Before going to bed, I knelt down [2] and prayed to God. I asked him to fulfil the promise of the Bible and deliver me. I had taken rum and tobacco, so I fell asleep and did not wake up until about three in the afternoon of the next day. When I awoke I was refreshed and cheerful. [3]

July 3. I thought often about the words in the Bible, *will deliver you*, but it seemed impossible that I should escape from the island. Then suddenly I said to myself, 'But I have been delivered from my illness!' God had delivered me, but I had not praised Him. Instead of thanking Him for saving my life, I had thought only of escaping from the island.

July 4. I began to read the Bible seriously. I decided to read a little every morning and every night. Now I understood the words *'Call on me, and I will deliver you'* in a different way. Before I had asked to be delivered from my island-prison. Now I asked to be delivered from the guilt of my sinful past. Deliverance from sin is a far greater blessing than deliverance from misery.

---

1. **deliver** : help and save.
2. **knelt down** : with both knees on the ground (to kneel - knelt - knelt).
3. **cheerful** : happy.

Robinson Crusoe

My mind was now calm and comforted. I had been on this unhappy island for more than ten months. I believed that no human being had ever come here before. I was lord of the whole island. If I liked, I could call myself king or emperor. I had enough wood to build twenty ships, enough food for an army. However, if I could not use it, it was of no value to me. I had enough to eat, so the rest was useless. I would have gladly given all my money for a little ink, because it would have been useful.

My life was now much easier than before. I thought much more about the blessings of my present life and much less about its misfortunes.

My ink had been gone for some time. My clothes were all worn out. [1] I made new clothes for myself from the skins of the goats I killed. This was very slow and difficult work, since I had no needle. The weather was so hot that I could have gone naked. However, I did not want to go naked, even though there was no one to see me.

I could not go naked, because the sun was so strong that it would burn my skin. I therefore made myself clothes, a hat, and

---

1. **worn out** : damaged by use or wear (to wear - wore - worn).

LORD OF THE ISLAND

even an umbrella. I tried to make a boat or canoe with which to escape from the island, for on a clear day I could see the mainland. It took me a long time to build the canoe. When it was finished it was too big for me to move. I could not get it to the shore, and so I left it where I had built it. Later, I made a smaller boat, but this was not large enough to take me to the mainland. I used it to sail around my island.

My life continued in this way for many years. It was an orderly life, filled with work and the praise of God. I was not unhappy. I was king of my island. My subjects were the goats, the dog, the cats, and some parrots I had tamed. There were no rebels [1] among my subjects. [2]

One day around noon something happened that changed my life on the island. I found the print of a man's naked foot on the beach. I stood and looked at the footprint [3] in amazement. [4] I looked around me but saw nothing. I went to higher ground and looked again, but it was the same. I saw no one, and no other footprint except that one. I

---

1. **rebels** : people who fight against the government.
2. **subjects** : members of a state except the king or queen.
3. **footprint** : print left by a foot on the sand.
4. **amazement** : great surprise.

was terrified, and went home to hide myself.

At first I thought it must have been the footprint of the devil, for how could a human being have come to this place? I then began to think the print was left by savages from the mainland. They must have come in canoes and left again. I was very thankful that they had not seen my boat.

How strange is the life of man! Today we desire what tomorrow we fear. For years I had desired human society. Now I was terrified at the thought that another human being had set his foot upon the island!

I thought again of the words in the Bible: *'Call upon me in the day of trouble, and I will deliver you, and you will praise me.'* I prayed to God to deliver me from danger. Afterwards, I opened my Bible and read, *Wait on* [1] *the Lord, and be of good cheer, and He shall strengthen* [2] *your heart.* Although these words comforted me, I was still afraid. Fear of danger is ten thousand times more terrifying than danger itself. I no longer trusted in God, as I had before. If I had kept my trust in God, I would have been more cheerful in this new distress.

---

1. **wait on** : follow, obey, worship.
2. **strengthen** : make strong.

1 **Complete these sentences using the Past Simple of the verbs given in brackets:**

a. Robinson (*shake*) .... the bag in the shadow of a rock.

b. It (*begin*) .... to rain.

c. When Robinson (*see*) .... the barley growing he (*think*) ....it was a miracle.

d. Robinson (*make*) .... a ladder to climb over the fence.

e. Robinson (*feel*) .... safe from any attack.

f. On April 16th there (*be*) .... an earthquake and a storm.

g. Robinson (*not/sleep*) .... all night because of a fever.

h. On June 26th Robinson (*kill*) .... a goat.

i. Robinson (*dream*) .... of a man descending from the sky who (*want*) .... to kill him.

j. Robinson (*awake*) .... terrified.

2 **Read pages 71-73 again, then match the correct parts of the sentences.**

a. Robinson had forgotten

b. Robinson had never thought before that his misfortunes

c. Robinson's father had warned him that God would not bless him

d. After eating some turtle meat

e. Robinson thought that nothing could happen

f. Robinson slept for a long time because

g. Robinson decided to read the Bible

h. Robinson prayed to God to be

1. without God's knowledge.

2. if he went to sea.

3. what his father had taught him.

4. Robinson asked God's blessing on what he was eating.

5. delivered from the sins of his past life.

6. every morning and night.

7. were the right punishment for his sins.

8. he had taken rum and tobacco.

3 **Discuss the following with your friends.**

    a. Do you think that Robinson was a rational/irrational man?

    b. Which means did Robinson use to face his difficult situation?

Write the adjectives in the sack under the right heading so as to define Robinson's personality.

egocentric
resourceful
individualistic
ambitious   capable
capable of building an empire
selfish   practical
enterprising

Qualities	Defects
....	....
....	....
....	....
....	....

Do you think that Robinson represents the ordinary man?
Why/Why not?

4 Simulation

Read pages 74-76 again. Imagine that you are Robinson and that you are going to be interviewed by your friend. Answer his questions.

INTERVIEWER: How did you feel on the island?

ROBINSON: ....
....

INTERVIEWER: Why did you make yourself some clothes, a hat and an umbrella?

ROBINSON: ....
....

INTERVIEWER: Why did you decide to build a canoe?

ROBINSON: ....
....

INTERVIEWER: How did you fill your time on the island?

ROBINSON: ....
....

INTERVIEWER: What did you find on the beach one day?

ROBINSON: ....
....

INTERVIEWER: What was your reaction to the discovery?

ROBINSON: ....
....

INTERVIEWER: What did you do to protect yourself?

ROBINSON: ....
....

Summary

Fill in the gaps in the summary using the linking words in the box.

> when   although   and   so   however
> but   after   afterwards   also   because
> then   as a result

One day Robinson found a small bag and decided to use it to store his gunpowder .... he shook it out near a rock. Soon .... the rains came and a month later he found barley and rice growing. Robinson thought it was a miracle and thanked God .... then remembered shaking the bag near the rock and felt less thankful. Soon after there was an earthquake and .... a great storm. .... Robinson was terrified, he never prayed to God. .... finding a large turtle Robinson fell ill .... prayed to God. The next day he woke up feeling better and he went and killed a goat .... he had no food. ...., he fell ill again and this time he had a dream about a man descending from the sky to kill him because he didn't repent of his sins. .... of this dream Robinson repented of his sinful life and started reading the Bible. His life became easier – he had lots of food and wood and he made some clothes, a hat and an umbrella from goat skins .... the sun was too strong to go naked. He .... built a canoe but when it was finished it was too big to move .... he left it where he had built it. .... Robinson found a man's footprint on the beach he was very frightened and went home to hide. He no longer trusted in God as he had before.

Mercantilism: [1] Trade, Wealth and Colonies

Daniel Defoe said: 'Trade is the wealth of the world. Trade makes the difference between rich and poor, between one nation and another.' In this short but significant [2] statement Defoe expressed the main ideas of the mercantilistic system that

Broad Quay, Bristol by unknown artist (early 18th century).

1. **mercantilism** : trade and commerce.
2. **significant** : important.

Britain was developing at the end of the 17th century.

The English mercantile spirit began during the Elizabethan Age when England realised that trade generated wealth. In the 1600s England's wealth was based on one main export – woollen cloth. By the end of the 17th century, when Daniel Defoe became a prosperous [1] London merchant, Britain had become the most important trading nation in Europe.

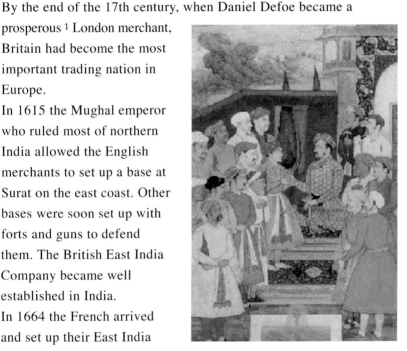

Jahangir, the Mughal emperor and his court.

In 1615 the Mughal emperor who ruled most of northern India allowed the English merchants to set up a base at Surat on the east coast. Other bases were soon set up with forts and guns to defend them. The British East India Company became well established in India.

In 1664 the French arrived and set up their East India Company. They too were interested in India's riches. Trade had become synonymous with [2] wealth, and this was the beginning of the great European power struggle in India as well as in North America. Coffee, the new drink from the Middle East, became popular in

---

1. **prosperous** : successful.
2. **synonymous with** : having the same meaning with.

Britain in the 1650s. By 1700 there were 2000 coffee houses in London where men met to chat, discuss politics and drink coffee. Daniel Defoe was a frequent visitor to the London coffee houses, where he went to enjoy the new drink, meet his friends and read the newspapers that circulated [1] there.

Tea was another new drink from India which became very popular particularly when it was sweetened with sugar from the Caribbean. Everyone liked sugar and almost everyone could afford to buy it. Sugar imports grew very quickly.

Sugar and tobacco were the most profitable products and both came from the New World where Britain had colonies. By 1700 the old enemy, Spain, had lost its power in the Caribbean. Britain took

A London coffee house, 1668.

1. **circulated** : passed something from one person to another.

control of several islands including Barbados and Jamaica, where sugar and tobacco grew.

Tobacco imports from the New World grew from 25,000 kilos in 1600 to 17 million kilos in 1700! Britain set up colonies on the Atlantic Coast of North America and controlled the lucrative tobacco trade.

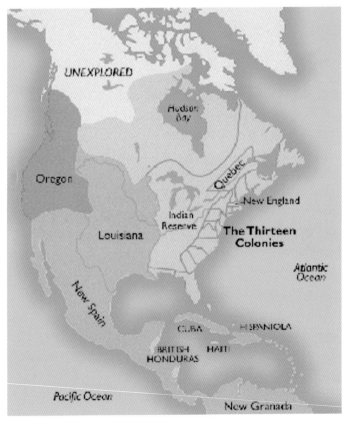

A map of North America in 1763.

The Wills Tobacco Company was a famous English company.

Tobacco and cotton plantations grew rapidly all over the southern American colonies thanks to slave labour. The north-eastern colonies, founded primarily by the English Puritans or Dissenters, did not use slave labour. These colonies had immense natural resources such as timber, [1] codfish and furs which were traded on a large scale. The Puritans were very hard workers and astute [2] merchants. They believed that mercantile transactions were determined by God who decided on everything in the world. Money through trade was considered a manifestation [3] of God's benevolence. [4] These American colonies accumulated a great amount of wealth through hard work and trade, which was later invested in industry.

England had begun to colonise the world, transforming faraway, sometimes primitive places into 'civilized', efficient trading posts that brought immense wealth to what was to become the British Empire – the biggest ever!

1. **timber** : wood.
2. **astute** : clever and quick to see how to benefit from a situation.
3. **manifestation** : a sign of something existing.
4. **benevolence** : kindness.

1 Decide if the sentences are right (R) or wrong (W). If there isn't sufficient information to answer, choose 'Doesn't say' (DS).

	R	W	DS
a. Defoe believed that slavery and trade generated wealth.	☐	☐	☐
b. The English mercantile spirit began during the Elizabethan Age.	☐	☐	☐
c. England and France were both interested in India's riches.	☐	☐	☐
d. The coffee plant originally came from Ethiopia.	☐	☐	☐
e. Coffee houses were popular meeting places for men in London during the 1700s.	☐	☐	☐
f. Everyone liked Caribbean sugar but it was a very expensive product.	☐	☐	☐
g. Tobacco and cotton were profitable products that grew in the southern American colonies thanks to the work of the colonists.	☐	☐	☐
h. The Puritans, who were hard workers, believed that money through trade was a sign of God's benevolence.	☐	☐	☐
i. The American colonies later invested their wealth in industry.	☐	☐	☐

Before reading

1 Fill in the blanks while listening to the first part of Chapter Four. Then check your answers by reading the text.

I had now been .... on the island for fifteen years. During all that time I had never seen another .... being. However, savages from the .... had clearly come to the island, and they might come again. I decided to build a second .... around my house and plant trees outside it, so that no one could .... In six years, I had a thick .... around my house.

About .... years after I saw the footprint, I thought I saw a .... in the distance off the western part of the .... Perhaps the savages from the mainland often came to that .... of the island. Perhaps God had guided me to the .... side, where the savages never came.

When I came down the hill to the shore, I was amazed and horrified to see human ...., hands, and feet lying on the .... There was a pit in the earth where a fire had been made. There the savages had made their inhuman ...., eating the bodies of their ....

I turned away from this terrible sight. I felt sick and vomited, then I .... back to my house.

My eyes were full of tears. I thanked God that I had been born a .... man, quite different from these savages. I thanked Him for the comforts. He had sent me in my ....

I thought I was probably safe from the savages. I had been on the island for .... years, and I had never met them. I could live there .... eighteen more years, if I did not choose to .... myself to them.

For two years after this, I stayed close to my house. Then I
.... to go about the island as before, but more
.... I did not fire my gun, for fear that the savages
.... hear the shot. Fortunately, I had my tame
........................, and could kill them for meat without ....
my gun.

I began to think night and day of .... some of these
savages. .... I could rescue their victim. I was horrified by
their .... feasting. I was full of anger towards them.
Sometimes I thought of burying five or six pounds of ....
under the place where they made their fire. When they
.... the fire, the gunpowder would .... and kill
them. But I did not want to use so much gunpowder, ... I
had very little ....

Then I thought of waiting for them, ... from sight, with
my guns loaded. In the middle of their .... feast, I would
shoot at them, and I would be .... to kill many. Then I
would run at them with my .... and sword. Even if there
were twenty of them, I was sure I .... kill them all. This
idea pleased me very much. I thought about it so much that I
.... to dream about it.

2 **Discuss the following question with your friends.**

Do you think Robinson will kill the savages? Why/Why not?

CHAPTER FOUR

FOOTPRINTS IN THE SAND

I had now been living on the island for fifteen years. During all that time I had never seen another human being. However, savages from the mainland had clearly come to the island, and they might come again. I decided to build a second fence around my house and plant trees outside it, so that no one could enter. In six years, I had a thick wood around my house.

About two years after I saw the footprint, I thought I saw a boat in the distance off the western part of the island. Perhaps the savages from the mainland often came to that side of the island. Perhaps God had guided me to the eastern side, where the savages never came.

Footprints in the Sand

When I came down the hill to the shore, I was amazed and horrified to see human skulls, [1] hands, and feet lying on the sand. There was a pit [2] in the earth where a fire had been made. There the savages had made their inhuman feast, [3] eating the bodies of their fellow-men.

I turned away from this terrible sight. I felt sick and vomited, [4] then I ran back to my house.

My eyes were full of tears. I thanked God that I had been born a civilized man, quite different from these savages. I thanked Him for the comforts He had sent me in my distress.

I thought I was probably safe from the savages. I had been on the island for eighteen years, and I had never met them. I could live there safely eighteen more years, if I did not choose to show myself to them.

For two years after this, I stayed close to my house. Then I began to go about the island as before, but more cautiously. [5] I did not fire my gun, for fear that the savages should hear the shot. Fortunately, I had my tame goats, and could kill them for meat without using my gun.

I began to think night and day of killing some of these savages. Perhaps I could rescue their victim. I was horrified by their inhuman feasting. I was full of anger towards them. Sometimes I

---

1. **skulls** : bony cases that enclose the brain.
2. **pit** : hole.
3. **feast** : large, special meal.
4. **vomited** : wanting to eject food through the mouth.
5. **cautiously** : carefully.

thought of burying five or six pounds [1] of gunpowder under the place where they made their fire. When they lit the fire, the gunpowder would explode and kill them. But I did not want to use so much gunpowder, since I had very little left.

Then I thought of waiting for them, hidden from sight, with my guns loaded. In the middle of their bloody feast, I would shoot at them, and I would be sure to kill many. Then I would run at them with my pistols and sword. Even if there were twenty of them, I was sure I could kill them all. This idea pleased me very much. I thought about it so much that I began to dream about it. *END*

Every day for two or three months I walked to the western side of the island and looked out to sea. All this time I was willing and eager to do an outrageous [2] act: I was ready to kill twenty or thirty naked savages. I had not given any thought to this sin. I had never asked myself if it were right or wrong. I was fired by my hatred [3] of their unnatural customs.

When I became tired of watching out for them every day, I began to question my plan. God had let them live unpunished for ages, and what had these people ever done to me? They did not think it was a sin to kill a prisoner and eat his flesh.

Then I thought that, though this custom was inhuman, it was really nothing to me. These people had done me no harm. If they

---

1. **five or six pounds** : about 2.5 kilos.
2. **outrageous** : horrible, shocking.
3. **hatred** : hate, strong dislike.

Footprints in the Sand

attacked me, then I might have the right to kill them. At present I was at no risk, and therefore I had no right to kill them. If I did so, I would be no better than the Spaniards, who had destroyed millions of savages in America. The savages had done the Spaniards no harm. All the Christian nations of Europe said that the Spaniards had been cruel and unnatural to kill those people.

These thoughts made me abandon my bloody plan. Besides, I thought that attacking them would put me at greater risk. If I did not kill all of them, the survivors would go home and return with others to kill me. Therefore, I decided, it was neither just nor wise to attack the savages.

I gave thanks to God that I had been saved from committing a great sin. For a year afterwards, I never went to the western shore except once, to get my boat and hide it on the eastern side of the island.

I had now been living on the island for twenty-three years, and I had found some pleasant ways to pass the time. I taught my parrot to speak. I taught him to say 'Poor Robinson Crusoe!' He lived with me for twenty-six years. Perhaps he is still living on the island, calling out 'Poor Robinson Crusoe!'.

I might have lived this way until I died contented [1] in old age, but God had other plans for me. How often in our lives the thing we fear most becomes the means of our deliverance! I could give many examples of this in my strange life. However, the best

---

1. **contented** : satisfied.

example is that of my
last years on the
island.

It was December
of my twenty-third
year. I went out early
one morning, when it
was still dark. Suddenly I saw
a fire on the shore about two

Footprints in the Sand

miles away. I went back to my house and pulled the ladder up after me. I loaded [1] all my guns and prayed to God to protect me.

After about two hours, I wanted to know what was happening outside. I climbed the hill behind my house, lay down in the grass, and looked towards the shore with my perspective glass. There I saw nine naked savages sitting around a small fire. They had two canoes with them. Some hours later, they got into their

1. **loaded** : put bullets into (past tense of the verb 'to load').

canoes and left the island. As soon as they were gone, I took my guns and went to the western shore. I saw that there had been three more canoes at that place. Looking out to sea, I saw them all rowing back to the mainland. Going down to the shore, I saw the remains of their unnatural feast: the blood, the bones, the parts of human bodies. I was so filled with anger at this sight that I began again to think about destroying the next savages who came there.

It was more than fifteen months before they returned to the island. During all this time I was in a murderous [1] state of mind. I did not think that, if I killed these savages, I would have to also kill the next ones who came, and the next, and the next. In the end I would be as much a murderer as they were, and perhaps much more so.

On the sixteenth of May in my twenty-fourth year on the island, there was a terrible storm. I was reading the Bible and thinking about my condition. Suddenly I heard the sound of a gun out at sea. I left my house and ran up to the top of the hill. There I saw a flash of fire on the sea and heard the sound of the gun again. 'It must be a ship in distress,' I thought, 'firing her guns to call for help.' I could not help them, but I thought that they might help me. Therefore I built a fire on the hilltop. I was sure that the people on the ship had seen my fire, because as soon as I lit it they fired the gun again.

---

1. **murderous** : extremely dangerous and likely to commit murder.

Footprints in the Sand

The next morning, I saw that the ship was wrecked. Perhaps the people on board were all dead. Or perhaps they had escaped in a boat and been blown away from the island towards the open sea. If so, they would die of starvation. Even now, they might be thinking of eating one another.

I was thankful that God had chosen to save me alone out of all those who had been drowned in this sea. But I was also sad, so that I cried out, 'Oh! If one person had been saved out of that ship and had escaped to this island, I would have had a companion, someone to talk to!' In all my time on the island, I never had so strong a desire for human society.

I was in great distress. 'Oh! If just one had been saved!' I cried over and over again. But it was not to be. A few days later I saw the body of a drowned boy come on shore, which made me very sad.

I took my boat and went out to the wreck. There I found no living soul, but I brought back more goods, about eleven hundred pieces of eight, and some gold. I stored these goods in a cave on the island.

For the next two years, I lived quietly and cautiously on the island. Yet all that time I was imagining ways to escape. Thus once again I was an example of the common weakness [1] of mankind: we are never satisfied with what God has given us, and this makes us miserable.

END

---

1. **weakness** : state in which a person lacks in physical or moral strength.

Robinson Crusoe

One night I dreamt I was going out in the morning from my house. Upon the shore I saw two canoes and eleven savages coming to land. They had with them another savage, and they were going to kill and eat him. Suddenly, their prisoner began to run as fast as he could. He ran to the thick woods in front of my house to hide himself. Seeing that he was alone, I showed myself to him. He knelt down before me and begged me to help him. I showed him the ladder and took him into my house. He became my servant. Then I thought I could go to the mainland with this man to guide me. I awoke full of joy, but when I found it was only a dream I felt very sad.

This dream gave me the idea that my only hope of escape was to get a savage. If possible I would rescue one of those they brought over to eat. This could only be done by killing all the other savages, and my heart trembled at the thought. However, my desire to escape was so strong that finally I decided to watch out for the savages again.

For about a year and a half I watched. No one came to the island in all that time. Then, one morning, I saw five canoes on the shore. I climbed the hill, hid myself in the grass, and watched them with my perspective glass. There were about thirty of them. They had built a fire and were dancing around it. As I watched, they brought two prisoners from the boats to be killed. One of the prisoners fell down, and the savages began cutting him up for their feast. At that moment, the other prisoner began to run. He ran with amazing speed along the shore towards my house.

Footprints in the Sand

I was terribly frightened when I saw him running towards me. I thought that all the others would follow him. My dream seemed to be coming true. When I saw that only three men were pursuing him, I felt less frightened. The prisoner came to the river, jumped in, and swam across. When his pursuers [1] came to the river, one of them stopped and turned back, for clearly he could not swim. The others swam across the river, but not so quickly as the prisoner had done.

I thought that God was calling me to save this poor creature's life. I thought that by saving his life I would get a servant, and perhaps a companion.

I took my guns and ran down to the shore. I cried out to the prisoner. At first he was frightened of me. Slowly I walked towards the two who followed. I hit the first one with my gun. Having knocked this fellow down, [2] I walked towards the other. I saw that he had a spear. He was ready to throw it at me. Therefore I had no choice but to shoot him.

Though he saw that both his enemies had fallen, the poor savage was frightened by the sound of my gun. I called to him and made encouraging signs. The poor creature was trembling. He walked towards me slowly. When he came close to me, he knelt on the ground and kissed the earth. He then put his head upon

---

1. **pursuers** : people who follow others.
2. **knocked ... down** : caused to fall by striking (past tense of the verb 'to knock down').

the ground. He took my foot and placed it upon his head. I helped him to his feet and encouraged him.

The savage I had knocked down now began to move. I pointed to him, to show my savage that his enemy was not dead. My savage spoke some words to me. I did not understand them, but I enjoyed listening to them. They were the first words spoken to me by any human being for over twenty-five years. I pointed my gun at the savage on the ground. My savage touched the sword at my side, as if asking to use it. I gave it to him, and he ran to his enemy and cut off his head with one blow. [1] When he had done this, he came back to me, laughing, and gave me my sword. Then he buried the bodies in the sand.

Afterwards, I took my savage to my cave and gave him food and water. I made signs to him that he should sleep, and pointed to the blanket where I often slept myself.

He was a strong handsome fellow, about twenty-six years old. He had a pleasant face, with all the sweetness and softness of a European, especially when he smiled. When he awoke he made many signs of thankfulness to me for saving his life. I showed him that I was pleased with him. Then I began to speak to him and teach him how to speak to me. First I told him that his name would be Friday, which was the name of the day on which I saved his life. I taught him to call me Master.

END

---

1. **blow** : hit, stroke.

Footprints in the Sand

I stayed with him in the cave all that night. The next morning we went out. We came to the place where we had buried the two men. Friday made signs to me that we should dig them up and eat them. I made signs of vomiting and let him know how much I hated the idea. I then led him to the top of the hill, to see if his enemies were still on the island.

The savages and their canoes were gone. We went down to the place where they had been. I was horrified at the sight, but Friday did not seem disturbed by it. The place was covered with human bones and blood. I saw three skulls, five hands, and the bones of three or four legs and feet. I made Friday put the skulls and bones into a pile and burn them. I could see that he still wished to eat some of the flesh.

When we had done this we went back to our house. I made clothes for Friday. Then I built a tent for him between the first fence and the second. Thus, Friday could not attack me during the night. But there was no need. Friday was the most faithful, loving, and sincere servant. He loved me as a child loves his father. He would have given his life to save mine.

God did not give all his creatures the knowledge of how best to use their capacities. [1] However, He gave all mankind the same reason, sentiments, and passions. It made me sad to think that God had hidden the saving knowledge from so many millions of souls. Someone like Friday would use that knowledge better than many white men.

---

1. **capacities** : abilities.

1 Look at the text on pages 92-93 again and underline the words which have the same meanings as the expressions listed below:

part	habits	presently
desired	started	right
action	persons	beach
without clothes	damage	but

Then state if they are:
NOUNS / ADJECTIVES / VERBS / ADVERBS / PREPOSITIONS

2 Read pages 93-96 again and write down suitable questions for the following answers:

a. ....?
He had been living on the island for 23 years.

b. ....?
'Poor Robinson Crusoe!'

c. ....?
For 26 years.

d. ....?
In December of his 23rd year.

e. ....?
Nine.

f. ....?
Some hours later.

g. ....?
Blood, bones and parts of human bodies.

h. ....?
Very angry.

i. ....?
To kill the next savages who came to the island.

3 **Listen to the section of the text on pages 96-97 and tick the correct answers following the statements below:**

a. There was a terrible storm

☐ after 16 months.

☐ the following day.

☐ on May 16th.

b. Robinson heard the sound of

☐ a gun.

☐ the water.

☐ thunder.

c. Robinson went to the top of the hill and built

☐ a hut.

☐ a fire.

☐ a gun.

d. The next morning the ship

☐ was safe.

☐ was sailing.

☐ was destroyed.

e. Robinson wished he could

☐ be dead.

☐ have a companion.

☐ go away.

f. A few days later Robinson saw

☐ the body of a drowned boy.

☐ a footprint.

☐ a fire.

g. Robinson went to the wreck and brought back

☐ goods.

☐ goods and gold.

☐ goods, money and gold.

h. Robinson lived quietly

☐ until he died.

☐ for the next two years.

☐ for the next two weeks only.

Check your answers by reading the text.

4 Scan the text on pages 98-99 and complete the following table.

What Robinson dreamt of one night	
Where the prisoner ran	
What the prisoner asked Robinson	
How Robinson felt when he awoke	
What Robinson saw one morning	
What the savages did to one prisoner	
What the other prisoner did	
What one of the followers did	
What Robinson did to the other followers	

5 Listen to the section of the text on pages 99-100 and decide whether the following statements are true (T) or false (F). Tick the correct column.

	T	F
a. Robinson called to the savage.	☐	☐
b. The savage hurt Robinson.	☐	☐
c. The savage placed Robinson's foot upon his head.	☐	☐
d. Robinson understood the savage's words.	☐	☐
e. The savage did not use Robinson's sword to kill his enemy.	☐	☐
f. Robinson buried the bodies in the sand.	☐	☐
g. The savage was thirty-six years old.	☐	☐
h. Friday showed signs of gratefulness.	☐	☐

Correct the false statements.

6 Now that the enemies are dead, what is Robinson going to do? Write down 5 sentences to express your expectations. Use *going to* in each sentence.

Eg. Robinson is going to teach the savage to call him master.

....

....

....

....

....

7 Focus on the savage's and Robinson's behaviour to each other and say:

a. what the savage did when he saw Robinson.

b. what attitude towards Robinson his actions showed.

c. what Robinson called the savage.

d. what Robinson taught the savage.

e. what Robinson's attitude towards the savage shows.

Summary

Read the summary and decide if the verbs should be in the Past Simple or Past Perfect.

Robinson .... (be) on the island for fifteen years and during this time he .... (never see) another human being. One day on the beach he .... (see) some skulls and human hands and feet. Cannibals .... (be) on the island! Robinson .... (thank) God for being civilized. He .... (think) about killing the savages but .... (realise) that if they .... (not attack) he .... (have) no right to kill them. After twenty-three years on the island he .... (find) more bones and human parts. Previously he .... (see) a fire and nine naked savages who .... (leave) in canoes. He .... (think) again about killing them. A year later there .... (be) a terrible storm and a ship .... (be) wrecked but there .... (be) no survivors. A few years later about thirty savages .... (come) to the island with two prisoners. They .... (kill) one of the prisoners but the other one .... (manage) to escape. Robinson .... (save) the prisoner and .... (take) him to his cave. Strangely Robinson .... (dream) about this event one and a half years earlier. Robinson .... (call) the savage Friday because he .... (save) him on that day of the week. Friday .... (become) his faithful servant.

Solitude[1] and Survivors in Literature

Shipwrecks, desert islands, solitude and survivors have fascinated writers and readers for centuries. A desert island or the heart of a jungle, where civilization does not exist, can symbolise a new start in life, a prison without bars, a longed-for paradise or a dreaded inferno. [2]

Many writers have contemplated what could happen to a human being who is forced to live in complete solitude, away from the society he/she is accustomed to. Will good or evil prevail in this individual?

In *Heart of Darkness* (1902) Joseph Conrad writes about Mr Kurtz, a European who goes to live in the heart of the Congo jungle far from civilization, and yields to his worst, most corrupt instincts.

Other writers such as Daniel Defoe and Jules Verne portray the sole survivor as a man whose better qualities prevail. Robinson Crusoe, the sole survivor of a shipwreck, relies on his faith in God, intelligence and Protestant upbringing which decrees

A mask from the Congo region.

1. **solitude** : the situation of being alone.
2. **inferno** : place like hell.

that the self-made man must depend on himself, his own hard work and ingenuity [1] in order to survive. In the novel, Robinson often mentions God and His divine will; he believes that being alone on the desert island is God's will. Defoe creates a situation where Robinson, who represents the 'civilized Western man', dominates Nature and sets up his 'colony' on the desert island. When he meets Friday he feels that Friday was meant to become his slave, or servant, and that he must be converted to Christianity.

Jules Verne.

A 19th-century edition of
Robinson Crusoe.

Jules Verne, the famous French author who wrote over one hundred years after Defoe, was greatly inspired by *Robinson Crusoe* when he wrote *The Mysterious Island.* In this novel a group of friends are stranded on a desert island and the theme of man's struggle to dominate Nature is again present. Just as Robinson Crusoe represents the intelligent, industrious, [2] God-fearing individual, Cyrus Smith, the intelligent, well-educated American engineer represents science and knowledge in *The Mysterious Island.*

1. **ingenuity** : cleverness and originality in solving problems.
2. **industrious** : hard-working.

In *The Mysterious Island* we find Nab, the freed black slave who is devoted to Cyrus Smith, his liberator and master. Nab is presented as the ideal servant: loyal, trustworthy and intelligent.

In Verne's other novel, *A Second Year Ashore*, he again confronts [1] the theme of young friends shipwrecked on a desert island and how they are able to survive. In this book Moko embodies the servant – a young black boy of fourteen who works on board the ship and does all sorts of odd jobs, but is never treated as an equal. Michel Tournier, the modern French author, was also inspired by *Robinson Crusoe* to write *'Vendredi ou la vie sauvage'*, 1971.

Robinson Crusoe and the footprint by Thomas Stothart, 1790.

Robinson and Friday.

1. **confronts** : deals with.

In this novel Friday is the protagonist [1] and the roles of the two men, Robinson and Friday, are reversed. [2] Friday is no longer the savage who needs to be 'civilized' and serve his master. Instead, Friday becomes Robinson's 'guide' and helps him establish a different, more creative relationship with Nature. Tournier shows us that there is much to be learned from a man like Friday, thus portraying [3] a completely new way of thinking.

1 What can a desert island or the heart of a jungle symbolise?

2 Fill in the table and compare how these authors portray the role of the sole survivor and his companion(s).

Author	Book	Sole Survivor	Companion (when applicable)
Defoe			
Verne			
Conrad			
Tournier			

3 What other famous writers have confronted this theme? Were they optimists or pessimists?

1. **protagonist** : one of the main characters in a story.
2. **reversed** : position being changed to its opposite.
3. **portraying** : representing.

Before reading

1 **What do you think Robinson will teach Friday? Choose some of the ideas in the box:**

> to read   to speak
> to build a shelter   to make bread   to cook
> to believe in God   to eat cooked meat
> to use a gun   to serve at table   to sing

2 **Read pages 112-114 and then answer the following questions.**

a. Why did Friday tremble?

....

b. What did Robinson Crusoe cook that night?

....

c. What did he teach Friday to do?

....

d. Whose nation ate the prisoners they took in battle?

....

e. Why would Robinson need a large boat?

....

CHAPTER FIVE

FRIDAY'S STORY

Friday learned to speak quickly. He was very pleased when he understood me or could make me understand him. It was good to talk to him. Now my life was easy. I took Friday out with me to shoot a goat. When I fired my gun, Friday trembled and tore open [1] his jacket to see if he were wounded. He knelt on the ground and said many things I did not understand. I think he was begging me not to kill him.

I took him by the hand and laughed at him, then pointed to the

---

1. **tore open** : made a split or a hole with a sudden pulling action (to tear - tore - torn).

FRIDAY'S STORY

goat I had shot. He was amazed. I believe that, if I had let him, he would have worshipped [1] me and my gun. For days afterwards he would not touch the gun, but he often spoke to it, begging it not to kill him.

That night I roasted some meat and gave it to Friday. He enjoyed it so much that he told me he would never again eat man's flesh. I was very glad to hear that.

The next day I taught Friday how to make bread. After a little time, he was able to do these things as well as I could do them myself. This was the best year of my life on the island. Now I had someone to talk to, and he was a pleasant fellow. [2] He was honest and simple. I began really to love him,  and I believe he loved me more than he had ever loved anything before.

One day I talked to Friday about his nation. I asked him what his nation did with the prisoners they took in battle.

'Do they carry them away and eat them, as these did?' I asked.

'Yes,' said Friday. 'My nation eat men too.'

'Do they ever carry prisoners to this island?'

'Yes. Sometimes.'

'Have you been here with them, Friday?'

---

1. **worshipped** : adored (past tense of the verb 'to worship').
2. **fellow** : man.

'Yes. I have been here.' He pointed to the western side of the island.

So Friday had been one of the cannibals [1] who used to come to the other side of the island. He told me that one time they had eaten twenty men, two women and a child.

Friday told me many things about the people of his nation and the nations nearby. Then he told me that at a great distance from his nation there lived white men like me, and that they had killed many people. I understood that these were Spaniards, whose cruelty was well-known.

I asked him if he thought I could go from this island to the place where the other white men lived. He said I could, but I would need a large boat. I began to hope that I could escape from the island, with Friday's help.

I taught Friday all I could about religion. One time I asked him who made him. He did not understand me at all. He thought I had asked who his father was. Then I asked him who made the sea, the earth, the hills, and the woods. He told me Benamuckee made them. Benamuckee was very old, much older than the sea or the land, Friday said.

'If this old person has made all things,' said I, 'why do all things not worship him?'

Friday looked very serious and said, 'All things say O to him'.

I asked what happened to the people who died in his country.

---

1. **cannibals** : people who eat human flesh.

Robinson Crusoe

He said they went to Benamuckee. Then I asked whether those they ate went to Benamuckee too, and he said yes.

I then began to teach him about the true God. I told him that the great Creator of all things lived up there (pointing towards heaven). I said He was omnipotent. [1] He could give everything to us and take everything away from us. Friday listened very attentively. He liked the idea that Jesus Christ was sent to save us and that God could hear our prayers. He said that if God could hear us in heaven, He must be a greater god than Benamuckee. Benamuckee only heard when people went to the mountains to speak to him, Friday said. He told me that only the old men were allowed to go to speak to Benamuckee. 'Well,' I thought, 'there are cunning [2] priests [3] even among the savages.'

I told Friday that the old men were not telling the truth when they said they had spoken to Benamuckee. I said perhaps they had spoken to the devil. I then had to explain to Friday who the devil was.

Some days later, I spoke to Friday about God again.

Friday said, 'If God is so strong, why does He not destroy the devil?'

I was surprised at this question. I was a very old man, but I was a very young teacher of religion. I asked him to repeat what he had said. This gave me the time to think of an answer.

---

1. **omnipotent** : able to do anything.
2. **cunning** : clever at cheating people.
3. **priests** : persons who perform religious duties.

Friday's Story

'God will punish the devil in the end,' said I.

That did not satisfy Friday. 'But why does God not kill him now? Why did God not kill him long ago?'

I said, 'Why does God not kill you and I when we are wicked? He gives us time to repent and be forgiven.'

Friday thought about this. Then he said, 'Well, well. I understand. You, I, and the devil are all wicked, but God lets us all live so that we can repent and be forgiven.'

Here I was in difficulty again, and I thought how true it was that reason alone cannot lead us to salvation. [1] I told Friday that I needed something and sent him to get it. This gave me time alone to pray to God that he would help me to teach Friday.

As a teacher, I had more sincerity [2] than knowledge. In trying to teach him, I taught myself many things that I did not know before and many I did not really understand. I wanted to understand more than ever before. I do not know whether I helped Friday, but I am sure that Friday helped me. I was more contented than before, and I enjoyed my home very much. I thanked God for allowing me to save the life and perhaps the soul of this poor savage. When I thought about these things I felt a secret joy, and I thanked God for bringing me to the island.

Friday and I lived happily together on the island for three years. The savage was now a good Christian, better indeed than I was myself. One day I showed him the wreck of the boat in which my companions and I had left our ship. Friday looked at it a long time then said, 'Once a boat like that came to my nation.'

---

1. **salvation** : (here) saving of a person's soul from sin and its consequences.
2. **sincerity** : honesty.

'Were there any white men in the boat?' I asked.

'Yes,' said Friday, 'there were seventeen'.

'And what happened to them?'

'They live in my nation,' he said.

Perhaps these white men were from the ship that I had seen wrecked near my island, I thought.

'But Friday,' said I, 'why do the people of your nation not kill and eat the white men?'

'We only eat the flesh of prisoners we catch in battle,' said he.

Some time after this, when we were on the hilltop looking out to sea, we saw the coast of America. 'Oh joy!' cried Friday. 'There is my country! There is my nation!'

His eyes shone and his face was eager. I began to worry. If Friday could return to his own nation, I thought, he would forget about me and his new religion. Perhaps he would even tell his people about me and return with hundreds of them to eat me.

I worried about this for several weeks. Then one day I asked him, 'Friday, would you like to return to your own nation?'

'Oh yes,' said Friday, 'that would make me very happy.'

'What would you do there?' I asked. 'Would you eat men's flesh and become a savage again?'

Friday shook his head and said, 'No. I would teach them how to live well and how to pray to God. I would teach them to eat bread and the flesh of goats and never to eat men.'

'But then,' I said, 'they would kill you.'

FRIDAY'S STORY

'No. They would not kill me. They would be willing [1] to learn.'

I told him that I would make a canoe for him to go back to his nation. Then Friday said that he would go if I would go with him.

'I go!' said I. 'But they would eat me!'

'No, no,' he said. 'I would tell them not to eat you. I would make them love you very much.'

I told him again that I would make him a canoe so that he could return to his nation. Friday looked very sad. 'Why are you angry with me?' he asked. I said I was not angry with him at all. 'Then why do you want to send me away?'

'But Friday,' said I, 'did you not say that you want to go home?'

'Yes, yes,' said Friday. 'I wish we were both there. I do not wish to return alone.'

'But what would I do there, Friday?' I asked.

'You could do a lot of good there. You could teach my people to be good. You could tell them about God.'

'No, no, Friday,' I said. 'You go without me and leave me here to live alone, as I did before.'

He looked very distressed at my words, and taking up a hatchet, he gave it to me and said, 'Kill me!'

'Why must I kill you?' I asked in amazement.

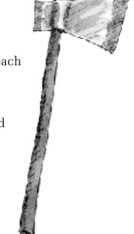

---

1. **willing** : ready, happy, enthusiastic.

'Why do you want to send me away? Do not send me away. It is better to kill me.' He spoke very sincerely, and his eyes were full of tears.

I saw clearly that he loved me and would never leave me. I told him that I would never send him away from me, if he was willing to stay.

We started building a boat large enough for the two of us and all our goods. The rainy season came before we finished the boat. Therefore, we brought it into the river to keep it safe until the weather was calm.

1 Simulation

Read the text on pages 114 and 116 again.
Robinson has asked Friday some questions. The following are
Friday's answers. Write Robinson's questions.

ROBINSON: ....?

FRIDAY: Benamuckee made them.

ROBINSON: ....?

FRIDAY: They go to Benamuckee.

ROBINSON: ....?

FRIDAY: Yes, they all go to Benamuckee.

ROBINSON: ....?

FRIDAY: Only when people go to the mountains to speak to him.

ROBINSON: ....?

FRIDAY: No, only the old men are allowed to speak to
             Benamuckee.

2 Read the text on pages 116-120 again, then answer the following
questions:

  a. What does Robinson think about the old men speaking to
Benamuckee?

  b. Why doesn't God kill wicked people, according to Robinson?

  c. Why can we see Robinson both as a teacher and as a learner?

  d. What did Friday remember when Robinson showed him the
wreck of the boat?

  e. Why weren't the men on the boat eaten?

  f. What would Friday do if he went back to his nation?

  g. Why did Friday think that Robinson was angry?

  h. What did they decide to do in the end?

Summary

Read the following summary and use the words below to fill in the gaps.

Robinson taught Friday to [1]............................. and he learnt
[2]............................. . He also taught him how to use a
[3]............................., to make [4]............................. and eat animal
meat. In particular Robinson tried to teach Friday about
[5]............................. and told him about [6]............................., good
and evil. In time Friday became a better Christian than
[7]............................. . They lived [8]............................. together for
[9]............................. years. One day Friday told Robinson that once
seventeen white [10]............................. had been shipwrecked and
had arrived at his nation. He explained that the savages didn't kill
and eat the white men because they only ate the
[11]............................. of prisoners they caught in battle. Friday said
he wanted to return to his own nation but would only go if
Robinson came with him. They started building a
[12]............................. big enough for the [13]............................. of
them and their [14]............................. .

1	speak / sing	9	ten / three
2	slowly / quickly	10	men / women
3	gun / knife	11	flesh / food
4	cakes / bread	12	boat / ship
5	religion / literature	13	three / two
6	Jesus Christ / Elton John	14	gold / goods
7	Robinson / the savages		
8	sadly / happily		

Juan Fernandez: Robinson Crusoe's Island

Daniel Defoe was probably inspired by Captain Woodes Rogers' *A Cruising Voyage around the World*, the book that told of the adventures of the Scottish sailor Alexander Selkirk, who asked to be left on the desert island of Juan Fernandez in 1704 after a quarrel with the captain of his ship. He lived on Juan Fernandez until 1709, when Captain Rogers and his crew rescued him.

The archipelago [1] of Juan Fernandez is located 674 kilometres west of Chile, surrounded by the tempestuous Pacific Ocean. It was

PACIFIC OCEAN

• PUERTO INGLES

Juan Fernandez   BAHÍA CUMBERLAND

.MIRADOR
ALEJANDRO SELKIRK

PUERTO
• FRANCES

Los Chamelos

Santa Clara

---

1. **archipelago** : a group of small islands.

123

discovered in 1574 by the Portuguese navigator Don Juan Fernandez, who was navigating for the Spanish Crown. For about 200 years the archipelago was the favourite hiding place of the most

Bahía Cumberland.

notorious [1] pirates of the time. The island had plenty of fresh water and timber, both necessary for pirate ships.

The terrible French pirate Jacob L'Hermite and others settled on the bay called Puerto Francés on the north-east side of the island. English navigators such as Anson, Cook, Davis, Rogers and Strong settled in Puerto Inglés. Recently discovered maps and documents of the 18th century tell us that in 1715 the Spanish captain Juan Ubilla hid an extraordinary [2] treasure of Inca gold worth about ten billion dollars on the

island. There are people on the island today who are looking for this extraordinary treasure!

1. **notorious** : famous for something bad.
2. **extraordinary** : very unusual and strange.

When the Spanish Crown had had enough of the pirates, they decided to defend the island by building seven forts and installing powerful cannons. During the second half of the 1700s the pirates had disappeared and the forts were abandoned. Both Spain and Chile tried to colonise Juan Fernandez but with no success.

This splendid [1] island has undergone very few changes since the 1700s. Today it belongs to Chile and there is a population of about 500 Spanish-speaking people, most of whom live in the village of San Juan Bautista, around Bahía Cumberland, and earn their living fishing for lobster and other fish.

Juan Fernandez is covered with cliffs of volcanic rock, steep mountains, lush tropical forests and moors. This remote [2] island is a

A hummingbird.

paradise for the Pacific sea lion and rare species of certain birds, such as the hummingbird. One hundred and forty-six species of plants grow on Juan Fernandez, of which one hundred and one grow exclusively on this island. In 1935 it became a national park and is now a part of Unesco's Wildlife Reserve. Nature lovers from all over the world come to enjoy the island's uniqueness.

Juan Fernandez can be reached by plane or by boat. In 1967 a landing strip was built allowing small planes to land. In 1993 the

1. **splendid** : impressive.
2. **remote** : isolated.

first phone line was installed thus improving communication with the rest of the world. The best way to move about on the island is on foot or by boat!

If you are planning a trip to Juan Fernandez, don't forget to visit:

a. the 'Casa de la Cultura Alfredo de Rodt y Biblioteca Daniel Defoe', which is open from Monday to Friday (free admission);

b. the cave where Selkirk lived;

c. 'Mirador de Selkirk', one of the highest points on the island, where Selkirk used to go to look for approaching vessels;

d. the remnants [1] of the 18th-century Spanish fort, Santa Barbara, with seven original cannons.

If you are not planning a trip to Juan Fernandez, view the island and find out more about Alexander Selkirk's adventurous life by visiting this web site:
http://www.ini.unizh.ch/~tobi/alex/alex.html

---

1. **remnants** : small remaining quantity of things.

1 Circle the correct words.

Alexander Selkirk was a *Spanish / Scottish* sailor who asked to be left on the desert island of Juan Fernandez.

In 1709 Captain Rogers and his crew *killed / rescued* him.

The *archipelago / peninsula* of Juan Fernandez is located in the *Atlantic / Pacific* Ocean, *west / east* of Chile. For about 200 years it was the hiding place of *terrorists / pirates*.

Today the island belongs to *Chile / Spain* and is part of Unesco's Wildlife Reserve, with *well-known / rare* animals, birds and plants.

Juan Fernandez can be reached by *plane or boat / car or train*.

2 Write what you know about each of these people.

a. Juan Ubilla ....
....

b. Jacob L'Hermite ....
....

c. Captain Woodes Rogers ....
....

d. Alexander Selkirk ....
....

Before reading

1 The words in the box are from Chapter Six. Use your imagination to complete the story. Then write it in your notebook.

> gun and sword   Spaniard   Friday's father
>
> king   cannibal   ship
>
> prisoners   captain   voyage   England

2 Read pages 129-130 and decide whether the sentences are true (T) or false (F).

		T	F
a.	Robinson had been on the island for twenty-seven years.	☐	☐
b.	Friday said he had seen three ships.	☐	☐
c.	Robinson gave Friday a big sword.	☐	☐
d.	Twenty-one savages and three prisoners landed close to his house.	☐	☐
e.	Robinson decided to attack them.	☐	☐

CHAPTER SIX

Coming Back Home

had now been on the island for twenty-seven years. One day I sent Friday to get a turtle. He came running back from the shore, crying, 'Oh, Master, Master! There are three canoes!' The poor fellow was terribly frightened.

'Will you help me to fight them, Friday?' said I.

'Oh yes,' said he.

'And will you do everything I tell you to do?'

'Yes, yes. I will,' said he.

'Then I will defend you, Friday,' said I, giving him a loaded gun and a hatchet.

He said, 'Master, I will die when you tell me to die.'

I took the pistols and my sword. We went up the hill to see

what was happening. There were twenty-one savages, three prisoners, and three canoes. They had landed closer to my house than ever before. This filled me with anger, but then I thought, 'What right have I to kill men who have done me no harm? It is a national sin, and God alone can punish the nations.' Friday could attack them, because they were the enemies of his nation. They had tried to kill and eat him. But, since they had done me no harm, I had no right to kill them. Therefore I decided not to attack them. Instead, I would hide myself and watch their cannibal feast. I would wait for a sign from God before I acted.

I sent Friday closer to look at the savages. He came back and told me that they were around the fire, eating the flesh of one of their prisoners. Another prisoner was lying upon the sand with his hands and feet bound. [1] Friday said that they would kill him

---

1. **bound** : tied up.

next. This made me very angry. Then Friday told me that this other prisoner was not of his nation. He was one of the white men who had come to Friday's nation in a boat. I was horrified at the thought of this white man waiting to be killed and eaten. I went closer and looked through my perspective glass. I saw a white man tied up on the beach. He wore clothes and was clearly a European.

I moved closer to the beach, keeping myself hidden behind the bushes. Two savages were approaching the poor Christian. They were going to kill him and bring him piece by piece to the fire. I told Friday to do as I did. I took one of my guns and aimed at the savages. Friday did the same. We both fired our guns at the same moment.

Friday was a better shot [1] than I. He killed two of them and wounded three more. All those who were not hurt jumped up and looked around in fear and amazement. I threw down that gun and took up another. Friday did the same. 'Are you ready, Friday?' said I.

'Yes.'

'Then fire, in the name of God!'

Again we both fired our guns at the same moment. Only two were killed, but many were wounded and ran about screaming and covered in blood. 'Come, Friday,' said I. 'Follow me'. I ran out of the bushes and showed myself to the savages. Friday followed me without question. I ran towards the poor victim. Some of the savages ran away and jumped into a canoe. I told

---

1. **shot** : someone who fires a gun.

Friday to shoot them. He killed two of them and wounded another.

I pulled out my knife and cut the ropes that bound the poor victim. I asked him in Portuguese what he was. He said, 'Espagniole'. I gave him a gun and a sword. The savages that remained had been very frightened by the sound of my gun. The poor creatures lay on the ground unable to move. The Spaniard took the sword and the gun very thankfully. They seemed to give him new strength. He attacked his murderers and cut two of them to pieces.

I told Friday to get the other guns. Then I sat down and began to load them. Friday and the Spaniard fought the savages. They came to me when they wanted a loaded gun.

Friday pursued the savages who were running away. He killed four of them with his hatchet. At the end of the battle, most of the savages were dead: – 3 killed at our first shot from the tree. 2 killed at the next shot. 2 killed by Friday in the boat. 2 killed by Friday of those at first wounded. 1 killed by Friday in the wood. 3 killed by the Spaniard. 4 killed by Friday while they were running away. 4 escaped in the boat, of which one was wounded or dead. 21 in all. –

Coming Back Home

I ran towards a canoe, because I wanted to pursue the savages who had escaped to sea. However, when I got to the canoe, I found another poor creature tied up in it. I cut the ropes that bound him and gave him rum to drink. Then I told Friday to explain to him that he was saved. But when Friday saw him, he kissed him. He cried, then he laughed, then he danced. I looked at him in amazement. 'Friday! What does this mean?' said I.

'Oh, Master!' said Friday, with tears in his eyes, 'that prisoner is my father!'

I was sincerely moved to see how much Friday loved his father. He got into the boat and took his father in his arms. There he stayed for half an hour, holding his father close. [1]

Friday took good care of his father and the Spaniard. He ran back to the house to bring them bread and fresh water. They were both very weak, and their feet hurt from being tied, so they could not walk. Friday put the Spaniard into the canoe beside his father. He pushed the canoe around the shore to our river. We carried them from the river to the house, but there we met a great difficulty. How could we get them over the fence? It was impossible, so Friday and I set to work. [2] In about two hours we

---

1. **holding ... close** : with arms around a person or thing.
2. **set to work** : started working (to set - set - set).

built a handsome tent for them, covered with sails, just outside the second fence.

My island was now peopled. I was the king, and all my subjects owed [1] their lives to me, because I had saved them all from certain death. Although I had only three subjects, they were all of different religions. My man Friday was a Protestant, his father was a pagan [2] and a cannibal, and the Spaniard was a Catholic. However, I allowed freedom of religion throughout [3] my country.

I said to the Spaniard, 'Do you think that the other white men who live in Friday's nation would like to escape to a Christian country?'

'Yes, they would,' said he.

'And would they swear loyalty to me and accept me as their leader?' I asked.

'They will be so glad to escape,' said he, 'that I am sure they will be faithful to you'.

I decided to send the Spaniard and Friday's father back to the mainland to speak to the other white men there. The Spaniard said that we should wait until we had enough food for them all. My grain and my goats were enough for four, but they would not be enough for sixteen others.

---

1. **owed** : were in debt (past tense of the verb 'to owe').
2. **pagan** : person who is not a believer in any of the world's main religions.
3. **throughout** : in every part.

Coming Back Home

We planted more barley and rice. I ordered Friday and his father to build a boat big enough for all of us. I told the Spaniard to supervise [1] their work. We went out to catch wild goats each day. I made Friday and the Spaniard go out one day, and Friday and myself the next, for we took our turns. In this way we got twenty young kids to breed [2] up with the rest.

When everything was ready, Friday's father and the Spaniard took a canoe and two guns and set off [3] for the mainland.

'If you bring others back with you,' said I, 'they must first swear loyalty to me.'

Eight days later, Friday awoke me crying, 'They are here! They are here!'

When I got to the shore, I saw the boat approaching us was not the one we expected. I told Friday to hide, because we did not know whether these people were friends or enemies. Then I went to get my perspective glass. I climbed to the top of the hill and looked out to sea. There I saw an English ship.

At first I thought an English ship must surely be friendly, then I had doubts. What was an English ship doing here, far from the English trading routes? I decided to be cautious. Now I am sure that those doubts were messages sent from God. If I had not been cautious, I would have been killed.

I saw the boat land on the beach. There were eleven men.

---

1. **supervise** : to direct and control.
2. **breed** : (here) to bring up and nourish (to breed - bred - bred).
3. **set off** : left for (past tense of the verb 'to set off').

ROBINSON CRUSOE

Three of them were bound with ropes. The three prisoners were crying out to the others, begging for mercy. Friday, who was by my side, said to me, 'Oh, Master! You see? Englishmen eat prisoners too.'

'No, Friday,' said I. 'They might murder them, but they will not eat them.'

At about two o'clock in the afternoon, the prisoners were left alone under a tree. The other men had gone into the woods to sleep. Friday and I took our guns and went down to show ourselves to the prisoners.

When I was very near to them but still hidden by the bushes, I cried out, 'Who are you, gentlemen?'

They were frightened by my voice, but they were even more frightened when I stepped out into the open. I was wearing my goatskin jacket and my hat. A naked sword hung by my side. I carried two guns and two pistols. I thought they were going to run away from me, so I said, 'Do not be afraid. I am your friend. How can I help you?'

One of them replied, 'You must be sent from heaven.'

'All help is from heaven, sir' I said. 'Now tell me what has happened.'

The poor man, with tears running down his face, said, 'I was the captain of that ship, but my men have rebelled against me.

Coming Back Home

They wanted to kill me, but I persuaded them to leave me on this island, with my two friends here.'

'Do your enemies have guns?' I asked.

He said they had only one gun with them and another in the boat.

'Well,' said I, 'it will be easy to kill them, because they are all asleep. But should we take them prisoner instead?'

He said that two of them were so evil that they must be killed, but that then the others would probably obey.

'If I save you, sir,' said I, 'you must promise to accept me as your leader and be faithful to me.'

He promised, and the other two did the same. Then I gave them each a loaded gun. They went into the woods towards the sleeping men. One awoke and cried out to the others. The captain's two companions fired their guns. They killed the two rebel leaders and took two prisoners. The others then begged for mercy.

With these repentant men, the captain went in the boat to the ship. Since the rebel leaders were now dead, the men on the ship decided to obey him once more. He then returned to the island and said to me, 'My good friend, there is your ship!'

These words affected [1] me greatly, and I sat down upon the ground with tears in my eyes. I did not forget to give thanks to God for delivering me. We asked the two rebel prisoners if they

---

1. **affected** : had an influence on (past tense of the verb 'to affect').

wished to be left on the island or to return to England, where they would be punished. They said they wished to stay on the island. Therefore, I showed them my house, my goats, my grain plantation, and my goods. I gave them guns and powder and wished them good fortune. [1]

And thus I left the island on the nineteenth of December 1686, having lived there for twenty-eight years, two months, and nineteen days. I was delivered on the same day of the same month that I escaped from slavery in Sallee.

I took with me my goatskin hat, my umbrella, and a parrot. I also took the money that had been so useless to me. After a long voyage, I arrived in England on the eleventh of June 1687, having been away for thirty-five years.

We had many adventures afterwards, my man Friday and I. I married and had three children, but then my wife died. A friend came home from a successful voyage, and he persuaded me to go in his ship to the East Indies. Our adventures on this later voyage may perhaps be the subject of another story.

THE END

---

1. **wished ... good fortune** : hoped for their success and happiness.

1 Complete the following table. One answer has been done for you.

What	Why
Robinson ran towards a canoe	to pursue the savages
Friday reacted in a strange way at seeing the creature	
Robinson and Friday built a tent	
Robinson allowed freedom of religion on the island	
More barley and rice were planted	
Friday's father and the Spaniard left for the mainland	

2 Tick the correct answer.

a. From the hilltop Robinson saw
☐ some boats.
☐ an English ship.
☐ land.

b. At the sight of the ship Robinson decided to
☐ be cautious.
☐ hide under a tree.
☐ welcome the ship.

c. Friday thought that the Englishmen were
- ☐ Christians.
- ☐ cannibals.
- ☐ enemies.

d. The prisoners were left
- ☐ in the boat.
- ☐ in a cave.
- ☐ under a tree.

e. The poor man who spoke was a
- ☐ priest.
- ☐ cannibal.
- ☐ captain.

f. The captain's two companions killed
- ☐ three men.
- ☐ two men.
- ☐ four men.

g. The two rebel prisoners decided to
- ☐ stay on the island.
- ☐ go back to England.
- ☐ run away.

h. Robinson left the island after living there
- ☐ nineteen years, twenty-eight months and two days.
- ☐ twenty years.
- ☐ twenty-eight years, two months and nineteen days.

i. Robinson took with him his
- ☐ goat and a parrot.
- ☐ goatskin hat, umbrella, parrot and money.
- ☐ parrot and money.

j. After his wife's death Robinson
- ☐ left for the West Indies.
- ☐ remained in England.
- ☐ left for the East Indies.

Summary

Read the summary and fill in the missing words.

One day after .... years more savages arrived with .... prisoners. Friday told Robinson that one of the prisoners was a .... man and so Robinson decided to .... They managed to free the white man who was a .... and the three of them shot and .... many of the savages. The others .... Then Robinson found another prisoner in a .... When Friday saw the man he ...., then laughed, then .... because the man was his .... So now on the island there were four people of different religions: Friday's father was a ...., Robinson and Friday were Protestants and the Spaniard was .... Robinson decided to .... the Spaniard and Friday's father back to the .... to go and bring the other white men to live on the island. Eight days later they saw a .... approaching but it wasn't the Spaniard with the other white men. It was an .... ship. Eight men arrived on the beach with three .... Robinson and Friday approached the prisoners and discovered that one of them was the .... of the ship and the other two his friends – his men had .... against him and intended to leave the three of them on the .... Robinson freed the men and they went and killed the two rebel .... The others .... for mercy. Robinson and Friday .... the island with the English ship after living there for over .... years. He took his goatskin ...., umbrella, parrot and .... with him. Six months later he arrived in England after having been away for .... years.

Final Activities

1 Jumbled order of events

The following is a list of the main events in the story. Number them to reconstruct the story: you will get a summary of the story.

☐ Robinson landed in Brazil and became a planter.

☐ Robinson got married and had three children.

☐ Robinson left his family and went away to sea.

☐ Robinson was shipwrecked on a remote island during an expedition to Africa.

☐ Robinson met Friday.

☐ Robinson left the island after about twenty-eight years.

☐ Robinson decided to leave for the East Indies.

☐ Robinson recorded what happened to him on the island in a journal.

☐ Robinson saved an English captain.

☐ Robinson arrived in England on 11th June 1687.

2 Themes

Answer the following questions, then find examples in the text to support your answers.

a. How did Robinson feel on the island?

....

b. What was his attitude as a coloniser?

....

c. What was Robinson's attitude towards the savages?

....

d. Do you believe that Robinson was a brave man?

....

e. How did Robinson react to cannibalism?

....

f. Was Robinson a religious man?

....

g. What was Robinson's attitude to God?

....

h. Why didn't Robinson yield to despair?

....

i. Did Robinson believe in freedom of religion?

....

j. Why is the religious feeling so present in the novel?

....

k. What was Robinson's attitude to Friday?

....

l. Did Robinson always treat Friday in the right way?

....

3 **Learning to appreciate style**

Tick as appropriate.

a. The story is narrated by
- [ ] a first-person narrator.
- [ ] a third-person narrator.

b. The narrator is
- [ ] the author.
- [ ] Robinson.
- [ ] another character.

c. The story is told from the point of view of
- [ ] Robinson.
- [ ] the author.
- [ ] another character.

d. The language is
- [ ] imaginary.
- [ ] ordinary and concrete.
- [ ] abstract.
- [ ] rich in poetic devices.

e. The tone is
- [ ] informative and didactic.
- [ ] ironical.
- [ ] neutral.
- [ ] supercilious.

f. The events narrated unfold
- [ ] in casual order.
- [ ] through a particular arrangement.
- [ ] in chronological order.

g. The reader is led to believe in 'everything' by
- [ ] Robinson's behaviour.
- [ ] the detailed descriptions.
- [ ] the exotic place.

Now find examples from the text to support your ideas.

Interpreting

4 **The book was interpreted in Defoe's times as a kind of prophecy of the future British Empire.**

According to that interpretation Robinson was the prototype of

☐ the colonised people.

☐ the colonising man.

☐ both the colonised and the colonising man.

Tick one answer and discuss your choice with your friends.

5 **Over to you**

a. Do you identify yourself with Robinson in his 'practical' attitude to life?

b. What did you like most in the story?

c. What didn't you like at all?

d. Has the story got any significance in the world today?

e. Did you like the end of the story? Why/Why not?

f. Imagine you have returned home after living on a desert island for 35 years. What would you do first? Do you think you would have difficulties in adapting to civilized life?

g. Think of a different ending, write it down in your notebook.

EXIT TEST

1 Context

Write a continuous passage stating:

a. who *Robinson Crusoe* was written by;
b. where and when he was born;
c. what you remember about his life;
d. what other works he wrote;
e. what the period he lived in was characterised by.

2 Comprehension

In a continuous passage explain:

a. what family Robinson belonged to;
b. why he went to sea;
c. how many voyages he made before he was shipwrecked;
d. what were the most striking experiences he had during these voyages and what he learnt from them;
e. how he reacted to being stranded on a desert island;
f. what he mainly missed there;
g. when he felt quite satisfied and contented.

3 Interpretation

Say:

a. what kind of man you think Robinson is (pessimistic/optimistic, active/passive, fatalistic cruel, generous... etc.);
b. if he may be considered a forerunner of modern entrepreneurs;
c. how much religious spirit is present in the novel and how religious Robinson himself is;
d. how he behaves to savages and natives;
e. what are the main theme(s) of the story and if there is a final message.

4 Key sentences

Who said ...?

a. 'It was a terrible storm.'
b. 'Do you call that a storm? ... That was nothing. Let's drink some rum and forget about it.'
c. 'Young man you, should never go to sea again.'
d. 'Poor Robinson Crusoe!'
e. 'Why do you want to send me away? Do not send me away! It is better to kill me.'
f. 'if I save you, sir ... you must promise to accept me as your leader and be faithful to me.'

Robinson Crusoe

KEY TO THE ACTIVITIES AND EXIT TEST

Daniel Defoe and his World

Page 16

1. **a.** autumn of 1660.
   b. was a Puritan, or Dissenter.
   c. considered the Plague a punishment sent by God.
   d. deeply influenced Defoe all his life.
   e. travelled throughout England, Scotland and Europe.
   f. the monarchs William and Mary.
   g. led him to bankruptcy in 1692.
   h. to publish his political newspaper, *The Review*.
   i. but not with the scholars of his epoch.
   j. the creator of the English novel as we know it today.

Page 18

1. *Open answers.*

2.

Date of birth	1632
Place of birth	York
Family conditions	good
His father's profession	merchant
Robinson's original surname	Kreutznaer
What happened to one brother	He became a soldier and was killed in a battle against the Spaniards
What happened to the other brother	Robinson does not know
Robinson's wish about the future	To go to sea

CHAPTER ONE

Page 34

1. **a.** If Robinson *remained* at home, his *life* would be pleasant.
   b. Only *desperate* men or *lucky* men went abroad.
   c. The *middle-state* was the best because a man could be *happy* and live in *peace*.
   d. Wise men *wished* to be neither *poor* nor rich.
   e. The *rich* and the poor suffered the *greatest* misfortunes.
   f. Moderation, *quietness* and good health were the *conditions* of the middle state.
   g. If Robinson went to *sea*, God would not bless him.
   h. Robinson would *be* sorry if he did not *follow* his father's *suggestions*.

2. **a.** he was moved by his father's words.
   b. persuade his father to allow him to go to sea.
   c. angry.
   d. one year later.
   e. a friend of his.
   f. were two storms on different days.
   g. scared.
   h. the ship sank.
   i. money.
   j. not to go to sea again.
   k. gentleman.

Page 35

3. **2** Robinson did not need to pay for

the voyage.

4 Robinson spent about forty pounds on things of little value which he would exchange for gold in Africa.

6 Robinson sold his gold in London.

1 Robinson met the captain of a ship that had been on the coast of Africa.

5 Robinson learnt how to be a good sailor and merchant.

3 The captain and Robinson became friends.

7 After his return to England, Robinson decided to do the same voyage again.

9 Robinson and the crew were made prisoners and taken to the port of Sallee.

8 The ship on which Robinson was travelling was attacked by the Turks.

10 Robinson was made a slave.

Page 36

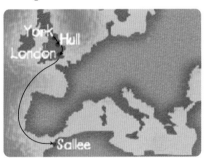

4. a. He was born in York.

b. From Hull.

c. The ship sank because of a storm.

d. Robinson went to London.

e. Robinson signed up for a voyage to Africa.

f. Yes, it was.

g. The ship was attacked by the Turks.

h. He was taken to the port of Sallee.

i. He was made a slave.

j. While fishing, Robinson pushed Ismael into the water and sailed with Xury to the African coast.

Page 37

5.

Place where they landed	All Saints' Bay, Brazil
What Robinson decided to be	a sugar planter
Why Robinson regretted selling Xury	because he needed help
What the captain of the Portuguese ship suggested to him	to ask a friend to send him some money
In which form Robinson got the money	in the form of English goods
What Robinson did with the money he got by selling the goods	he bought himself a Negro slave
How long Robinson took to learn the language	four years
Main problem about slaves in Brazil	there were very few and cost a lot of money
What the planters asked Robinson to do	to go with them to Africa to buy slaves

6. a. When *did the ship leave?*

b. When *did a hurricane hit their ship?*

c. What *was the weather like after 12 days?*

d. What *happened while sailing to Barbados?*

e. Why *did the boat turn over?*

f. What *carried Robinson towards the shore?*

g. Where *did Robinson lie down?*

Summary

Page 38

was born – desire – sea – nineteen – Hull – storms – sink – rescued – signed up – sailor – merchant – voyage – pursued – prisoners – slavery – escape – approached – Portuguese – Brazil – sold – sugar planter – prosperous – buy – left – September – turned over – swim

The Slave Trade

Page 43

1. **a.** commodity
    b. lucrative
    c. African slaves
    d. survived, journey, plantation
    e. colonies, east
    f. triangular, sugar cane, rum
    g. Tobacco, cotton, South
    h. abolished

Page 44

1. *Open answer.*

CHAPTER TWO

Page 58

1. **a.** true
    b. true
    c. false – He had no gun.
    d. false – He slept in a tree.
    e. false – The sun was shining.
    f. true
    g. false – He made a raft.
    h. true
    i. true
    j. false – He made a tent.
    k. false – He took the money.
    l. true

Page 59

2. *Open answer.*

3. **a.** he wanted to protect himself from savages and wild animals.
    b. any ship coming near the island could be seen.
    c. flat shelf / nothing could attack him from behind.
    d. tent / it was sheltered from the sun all day.
    e. fence / protect himself.
    f. ladder / bring the ladder in and protect himself from men and beasts.
    g. he needed a place to store his property.

Page 60

4. *Possible answers:*

Things that Robinson brought from the ship	Use Robinson made of them
eg.: hatchets	to make a fence, to cut wood
pieces of wood	to make a raft, a fence etc.
food	to eat
clothes	to dress himself/keep himself warm
guns/bullets	to shoot animals/protect himself
blankets	to keep warm at night
sails	to make the tent
hammock	to sleep comfortably

Things that Robinson made for himself on the island	Use Robinson made of them
eg.: ladder	to climb over the fence
tent	to be sheltered from the sun
wooden fence	to protect himself
cave	to store his property

5. **a.** Because he was alone on an island.
    b. Because he had survived and was well-equipped.
    c. He planted a wooden cross and made a cut every day.
    d. He had taken three Bibles and some Catholic prayer books.
    e. He had taken two cats and one dog.
    f. He made a list of comforts and miseries.

Page 61

6.

Negative Aspects	Positive Aspects
– he had no means of defending himself	– but there were no wild beasts on the island
– he had no clothes	– but the weather was hot
– he had no soul to speak to	– but he had been able to supply himself with many things
– he felt singled out to lead this miserable life	– but he hoped God would save him
– he was alone	– but he was not starving
– he was stranded on an island	– but he was alive

7. *Open answer.*

Page 62

8. **1** Robinson was shipwrecked on an island which he called the Island of Despair on September 30, 1659.
   4 Robinson shot a she-goat.
   7 Robinson killed two birds.
   3 The bad weather broke the ship into pieces.
   5 Robinson set up his tent and hammock.
   8 Robinson started to plan his time.
   9 Robinson made himself a chair.
   2 Robinson got all he could out of the ship.
   10 Robinson started to dig in the rock to make a cave.
   6 Robinson built a fence around his tent.

9. a. cave
   b. store
   c. wooden
   d. supply
   e. starvation
   f. sheltered
   g. gunpowder

Summary

Page 63

The following words should be inserted:

tree – ship – hammock
tent – hill – fence
cliff – gunpowder
knife – journal – goats

Shipwrecks!

Page 66

1. a. Shipwrecks and pirate attacks.
   b. **Physical hardships:** malnutrition, scurvy, illness, serious injuries and amputation of an arm or limb by the ship's surgeon.

Psychological hardships: being far from home, not being able to see land for months at a time and living in extremely crowded and often dirty living quarters.
   c. Marine archaeologists.
   d. *Suggested answer:* The sea is very rough. There is a shipwreck near the beach. The masts of the ship are missing, probably due to the violence of the storm. Some people are in the water trying to reach the shore, from where many others are watching the terrible sight.

Page 67

1. a. A little bag that had once held grain on board his ship.
   b. Gunpowder.
   c. English barley and rice.
   d. He thought it was a miracle; that God had made it grow there to comfort him.
   e. He saved the grain to plant it again.
   f. He could climb over the fence.
   g. Because the earth came falling down from the roof of his cave.
   h. It was an earthquake.
   i. Three hours.

CHAPTER THREE

Page 78

1. a. shook
   b. began
   c. saw; thought
   d. made
   e. felt
   f. was
   g. did not sleep
   h. killed
   i. dreamt/dreamed; wanted
   j. awoke

2. a. 3 **b.** 7 **c.** 2 **d.** 4
   e. 1 **f.** 8 **g.** 6 **h.** 5

Page 79

3. a. Robinson was a rational man.

b. Robinson faced his difficulties by using common sense and his deep faith in God.

Qualities	Defects
capable	ambitious
capable of building	selfish
an empire	egocentric
practical	individualistic
resourceful	
enterprising	

Suggested answer:
Robinson certainly represents the ordinary man because he has the qualities and defects mentioned above.

Page 80

4. **Interviewer:** How did you feel on the island?
Robinson: I felt like the lord of the island.
Interviewer: Why did you make yourself some clothes, a hat and an umbrella?
Robinson: To protect myself from the sun.
Interviewer: Why did you decide to build a canoe?
Robinson: In order to escape.
Interviewer: How did you fill your time on the island?
Robinson: I filled my time with work and the praise of God.
Interviewer: What did you find on the beach one day?
Robinson: I found a man's footprint.
Interviewer: What was your reaction to the discovery?
Robinson: I was terrified.
Interviewer: What did you do to protect yourself?
Robinson: I went home and hid myself.

Summary

Page 81

so – afterwards – but – then – Although – After – and – because – However – As a result – because – also – so – When

Mercantilism: Trade, Wealth and Colonies

Page 87

1. a. W   **b.** R
   c. R   **d.** DS
   e. R   **f.** W
   g. W   **h.** R
   i. R

Page 88

1. (The answers can be checked by reading the text.)

Page 89

2. *Open answer.*

CHAPTER FOUR

Page 102

1. part = side *(noun)*
desired = was willing *(verb)*
action = act *(noun)*
without clothes = naked *(adjective)*
habits = customs *(noun)*
started = began *(verb)*
persons = people *(noun)*
damage = harm *(noun)*
presently = at present *(adverb)*
right = just *(adjective)*
beach = shore *(noun)*
but = except *(preposition)*

2. a. How long had Robinson been living on the island?
   b. What could his parrot say? / What did he teach his parrot to say?
   c. How long did the parrot stay with him?
   d. When did Robinson see a fire on the shore?

e. How many savages were there?
f. When did they leave the island?
g. What did Robinson see on the beach?
h. How did Robinson feel?
i. What did he start to think of?

Page 103

3. **a.** on May 16th.
   b. a gun.
   c. a fire.
   d. was destroyed.
   e. have a companion.
   f. the body of a drowned boy.
   g. goods, money and gold.
   h. for the next two years.

Page 104

4.

What Robinson dreamt of one night	Robinson dreamt he saw some savages on the beach with a prisoner.
Where the prisoner ran	The prisoner ran to the thick woods in front of Robinson's house.
What the prisoner asked Robinson	The prisoner asked Robinson to help him.
How Robinson felt when he awoke	Robinson felt happy.
What Robinson saw one morning	Robinson saw five canoes on the shore.
What the savages did to one prisoner	They started cutting him up for their feast.
What the other prisoner did	The other prisoner began to run towards Robinson's house.
What one of the followers did	One of the followers stopped chasing the prisoner because he could not swim and so couldn't cross the river.
What Robinson did to the other followers	Robinson hit one of them with his gun and shot the other.

Page 105

5. **a.** true

b. false – The savage didn't hurt Robinson.
c. true
d. false – Robinson didn't understand the savage's words.
e. false – The savage used Robinson's sword to kill his enemy.
f. false – The savage buried the bodies in the sand.
g. false – The savage was about twenty-six years old.
h. true

6. *Open answer.*

7. **a.** The savage put his head on the ground and put Robinson's foot on his head.
   b. His actions showed that he was very grateful.
   c. Robinson called the savage Friday.
   d. Robinson taught the savage how to speak and to call him master.
   e. Robinson's attitude towards the savage shows that he feels superior to him.

Summary

Page 106

had been – had never seen – saw – had been – thanked – thought – realised – did not attack – had – found – had seen – had left – thought – was – was – were – came – killed – managed – saved – took – had dreamt – called – had saved – became

Solitude and Survivors in Literature

Page 110

1. A desert island or the heart of a jungle can symbolise a new start in life, a prison without bars, a longed-for paradise or a dreaded inferno.

2.

Author	Book	Sole Survivor	Companion (when applicable)
Defoe	'Robinson Crusoe'	Robinson Crusoe	Friday, who becomes his servant/slave
Verne	'Mysterious Island'	Cyrus Smith	Nab, the freed slave devoted to his master
Conrad	'Heart of Darkness'	Mr Kurtz	(Not applicable)
Tournier	'Vendredi ou la vie Sauvage'	Robinson Crusoe	Friday, who becomes Robinson's guide and helps him to establish a better relationship with Nature.

3. Suggested answer:
William Shakespeare confronted this theme in his play *The Tempest* and he seemed to be more of a pessimist than an optimist.

Page 111

1. *Open answers.*

2. a. Because Robinson fired his gun.
   b. Roasted meat.
   c. He taught him how to make bread.
   d. Friday's nation.
   e. To go from his island to the island where other white men lived.

CHAPTER FIVE

Page 121

1. Robinson: Who made the sea, the earth, the hills and the woods?
Friday: Benamuckee made them.
Robinson: What happens to the people who die in your country?
Friday: They go to Benamuckee.
Robinson: Do all the people you eat go to Benamuckee too?
Friday: Yes, they all go to Benamuckee.
Robinson: When does Benamuckee listen to people?
Friday: Only when people go to the mountains to speak to him.
Robinson: Is everyone allowed to speak to Benamuckee?
Friday: No, only the old men are allowed to speak to Benamuckee.

2. a. Robinson thinks they are cunning.
   b. To give them time to repent and be forgiven.
   c. Because, by teaching Friday, he learns things he did not know before.
   d. Friday remembered that a boat like that had come to his nation once.
   e. Because they hadn't been caught in battle.
   f. He'd teach his people how to pray to God and not to eat men.
   g. Because Friday thought that Robinson would send him away.
   h. They decided to stay together and they built a boat for the two of them.

Summary

Page 122

1. speak
2. quickly
3. gun
4. bread
5. religion
6. Jesus Christ
7. Robinson
8. happily
9. three
10. men
11. flesh
12. boat
13. two
14. goods

Juan Fernandez: Robinson Crusoe's Island

Page 127

1. Scottish, rescued, archipelago, Pacific, west, pirates, Chile, rare, plane or boat

2. **a.** In 1715 the Spanish captain Juan Ubilla hid an extraordinary treasure of Inca gold on the island.
   b. Jacob L'Hermite was a terrible French pirate who settled on the bay called Puerto Frances.
   c. Captain Woodes Rogers wrote *A Cruising Voyage around the World*, the true story of the adventures of the Scottish sailor, Selkirk.
   d. Alexander Selkirk was a Scottish sailor who asked to be left on the desert island of Juan Fernandez in 1704 following a quarrel with the captain of the ship. He lived on the island until 1709.

Page 128

1. *Open answers.*

2. **a.** T / **b.** F / **c.** F / **d.** T / **e.** F

CHAPTER SIX

Page 140

1.

What	Why
Robinson ran towards a canoe	to pursue the savages
Friday reacted in a strange way at seeing the creature	because the creature was his father
Robinson and Friday built a tent	for the Spaniard and Friday's father
Robinson allowed freedom of religion on the island	because one of his subjects was Catholic, one was Protestant and one Pagan
More barley and rice were planted	to have enough food for the other people from the mainland
Friday's father and the Spaniard left for the mainland	to bring back the other white people.

2. **a.** an English ship.
   b. be cautious.
   c. cannibals.
   d. under a tree.
   e. captain.
   f. two men.
   g. stay on the island.
   h. twenty-eight years, two months and nineteen days.
   i. goatskin hat, umbrella, parrot and money.
   j. left for the East Indies.

Summary

Page 142

27 – 3 – white – attack – Spaniard – killed – escaped – canoe – cried – danced – father – pagan – Catholic – send – mainland – ship – English – prisoners – captain – rebelled – island – leaders – begged – left – 28 – hat – money – 35

Final Activities

Page 143

1. 2. Robinson landed in Brazil and became a planter.
   9. Robinson got married and had three children.
   1. Robinson left his family and went away to sea.
   3. Robinson was shipwrecked on a remote island during an expedition to Africa.
   5. Robinson met Friday.
   7. Robinson left the island after about twenty-eight years.
   10. Robinson decided to leave for the East Indies.
   4. Robinson recorded what happened to him on the island in a journal.
   6. Robinson saved an English captain.
   8. Robinson arrived in England on 11th June 1687.

Page 144

2. *Possible answers:*

a. He felt like an emperor, the lord of the island, but he also felt lonely at times.
b. His was the typical attitude of the coloniser: that his customs and way of life were superior to those of the colonised people.
c. Robinson felt superior to the savages.
d. Yes, Robinson was a brave man: he faced all circumstances on his own!
e. He was disgusted by it and taught Friday not to do it.
f. At the beginning no. But after being stranded on the island he found his faith in God again and found comfort in the Bible and in prayer.
g. Sometimes he thought that God had forgotten him, but most of the time he prayed and certainly confided in God.
h. According to the Puritan idea, despair meant lack of confidence in God's providence.
i. Yes, he did. He allowed freedom of religion on the island with his three 'subjects'.
j. The religious feeling is so present because the book also aims at teaching a moral.
k. The attitude of a teacher and an educator.
l. No, he didn't. Nobody is perfect!

Page 145

3. a. a first-person narrator.
   b. Robinson.
   c. Robinson.
   d. ordinary and concrete.
   e. informative and didactic.
   f. in chronological order.
   g. the detailed descriptions.

Page 146

4. both the colonised and the colonising man

5. *Open answers.*

1

a. Daniel Defoe.

b. He was born in London in 1660.

c. He was brought up in a Dissenting or Puritan family. He was a merchant and initially had success, but became bankrupt in 1692 after some risky business ventures. After this he became more interested in journalism and began publishing political pamphlets and a political newspaper, *The Review*. He published *Robinson Crusoe* in 1719 and it was immediately successful.

d. His other works include: *The Farther Adventures of Robinson Crusoe, Moll Flanders* and *Roxana*.

e. He lived in a pre-industrial society that was beginning to expand rapidly.

2

a. A merchant family.

b. Because it was his only desire.

c. 3

d. During his first voyage there were several bad storms and Robinson was very sick and frightened. His second voyage was very successful and he made some money. His third voyage finished badly as they were taken prisoner by Turkish pirates.

e. At the beginning he was thankful to God for having survived the shipwreck. Then he feels desperate when he realises his terrible situation. However, he soon becomes very enterprising: he saves what he can from the shipwreck and makes himself a house.

f. Human company.

g. After about 10 months on the island. His days are full of work and prayer.

3

a. Optimistic and active.

b. Yes, he is very enterprising.

c. The theme of religion runs through the whole novel. At the beginning Robinson is not particularly religious but this changes gradually until a lot of his time is taken up with prayer and Bible reading.

d. His behaviour can be compared to that of the Imperial British. Although the island is not his, he behaves as if he is the master of the island and superior to the natives.

e. The main themes are: religion and colonisation.

4

a. Robinson

b. Robinson's friend

c. The captain of the ship on Robinson's first voyage.

d. Robinson and his parrot

e. Friday

f. Robinson

NOTES

Black Cat English Readers

BLACK CAT ENGLISH CLUB
Membership Application Form

BLACK CAT ENGLISH CLUB is for those who love English reading and seek for better English to share and learn with fun together.

Benefits offered:
- *Membership Card*
- *Member badge, poster, bookmark*
- *Book discount coupon*
- *Black Cat English Reward Scheme*
- *English learning e-forum*
- *Surprise gift and more...*

Simply fill out the application form below and fax it back to **2565 1113**.

Join Now! It's FREE exclusively for readers who have purchased *Black Cat English Readers* !

The book(or book set) that you have purchased: _____

English Name: _____ (Surname) _____ (Given Name)

Chinese Name: _____

Address: _____

Tel: _____ Fax: _____

Email: _____
(Login password for e-forum will be sent to this email address.)

Sex: ❏ Male   ❏ Female

Education Background: ❏ Primary 1-3   ❏ Primary 4-6   ❏ Junior Secondary Education (F1-3)
❏ Senior Secondary Education (F4-5)   ❏ Matriculation
❏ College   ❏ University or above

Age: ❏ 6 - 9   ❏ 10 - 12   ❏ 13 - 15   ❏ 16 - 18   ❏ 19 - 24   ❏ 25 - 34
❏ 35 - 44   ❏ 45 - 54   ❏ 55 or above

Occupation: ❏ Student   ❏ Teacher   ❏ White Collar   ❏ Blue Collar
❏ Professional   ❏ Manager   ❏ Business Owner   ❏ Housewife
❏ Others (please specify: _____)

As a member, what would you like **BLACK CAT ENGLISH CLUB** to offer:
❏ Member gathering/ party   ❏ English class with native teacher   ❏ English competition
❏ Newsletter   ❏ Online sharing   ❏ Book fair
❏ Book discount   ❏ Others (please specify: _____)

Other suggestions to **BLACK CAT ENGLISH CLUB**:

_____

Please sign here: _____

(Date: _____)